Praise for TONY DUNB the Tubby Dubonnet ser

"Hair-Raising... Dunbar revels in the raffish charm and humor of his famously rambunctious city."

—*The New York Times Book Review*

"Dunbar has an excellent ear for dialogue... His stylish take on Big Easy lowlife is reminiscent of the best of Donald Westlake and Elmore Leonard."

—*Booklist*

"Dunbar catches the rich, dark spirit of New Orleans better than anyone."

—*Publishers Weekly*

"Take one cup of Raymond Chandler, one cup of Tennessee Williams, add a quart of salty humor, and you will get something resembling Dunbar's crazy mixture of crime and offbeat comedy."

—*The Baltimore Sun*

"The literary equivalent of a *film noir*—fast, tough, tense, and darkly funny... so deeply satisfying in the settling of the story's several scores that a reader might well disturb the midnight silence with laughter."

—*Los Angeles Times Book Review*

NIGHT WATCHMAN

A Tubby Dubonnet Mystery

BY

TONY DUNBAR

booksBnimble Publishing
New Orleans, La.

Night Watchman

This book is available in both mobi and print formats.

eBook ISBN: 978-0-9861783-2-0
Print ISBN-13: 978-0-9861783-4-4

www.booksbnimble.com

First booksBnimble electronic publication: April, 2015

Print layout by eBooks By Barb for Booknook.biz

Dedication

To Nancy, eternally mysterious

I

Under baby blue skies, Tubby's eyes roamed over a harbor full of brightly colored sailboats, looking for imperfections. There weren't any. The sea on the horizon was flat, and the little specks of pleasure boats out beyond the pass powered across water smooth as silk under clouds like cotton balls. The harbor was framed by colorful minarets, tall condo towers, air-conditioned castles stacked high with balconies overlooking all the splendid water. Just like the balcony on which he sat, in a burnished aluminum chair tightly covered in bright yellow fabric. He was sipping a Beefeaters on ice. It was nice.

A tree-covered park below him surrounded a marina, which was neatly packed with vessels, sails furled, in repose. Sprinkled among the trees were civic artworks and popular amusements, including a canteen for selling beer and ice cream, about which children and adults clustered. The spacious public lawns were dotted with young parents, blankets on the ground, and their scampering infants.

Tubby beheld it all and lifted his heavy glass. He took a deep drink. Droplets of condensation fell onto his pants. This was, he could confirm, the most beautiful, sunny, sophisticated city on the Gulf of Mexico. Naples, Florida. It was created and must exist for no purpose but to make people happy.

"Happier by far if you have considerable assets," he said out loud, not realizing he had done so.

All of the happiest citizens had them, assets that was. These citizens made up a majority, at least as far as this visiting tourist from New Orleans could tell, of the overall population. In any case the real people seemed to make their money feeding, watering, caring for, and selling land to the fortunate ones who had the scratch.

It was, however, quite hot here in August, reminiscent of New Orleans. Many people, he had observed, spent their days inside.

Two planes buzzed overhead, advertising Banana Tanning Oil on long banners trailing from their tails. They had taken off further inland and were off to crisscross the island beaches, hawking their beachy wares.

He watched the planes disappear behind the condo towers, through the tresses of extremely beautiful bromeliads. They hung from the roof over his head, which was itself the floor of an identical balcony above. Their orange and flaming red flowers, surrounded by tiger-striped fronds, begged, he imagined, to be pollinated. The sun was warm on his sandaled toes.

"I'm drinking again," he observed to no one in particular and rose to go inside through the sliding doors.

All of the others, there were seven, had vodka, with olives or fruity flavors. He freshened his own drink in the kitchen and walked back through the party, winking at Marguerite in passing, and then went back to his balcony to shut them out again. A boat horn sounded across the harbor, signaling something a-coming from far away.

Even if you were hidden behind the balcony's flowers, it was so bright outside you couldn't open your eyes unless you were prepared to squint hard at the world. A beautiful tropical world it was, however, lush, though also quite spotless and clean. No question, things were good here. The Recession was over and high real estate prices had returned.

"Tubby, our guests are about to leave," Marguerite interrupted from the space she had just created by sliding open the glass door, emitting a welcome gust of chill air. "Won't you come inside?" She looked at him anxiously and hopefully, her red hair a halo.

Taking his drink along, he rejoined the party for the farewells. Though he was lost in the fog of gin and his own thoughts, he picked up the tail-end of a conversation. It was about a homicide victim, Trayvon Martin, an unarmed black youth who had been pursued down the sidewalk of a nearby town by an armed neighbor. A fight ensued, and the neighbor killed the boy, claiming the protection of Florida's "stand-your-ground" law.

"He just shot him for no reason," said one of the guests, a pert retired interior decorator whose short hair was dyed a dark luminescent brown.

This little fragment of a conversation triggered a tiny click in his mind, which inexplicably sent him back to when he was a teenager, back to a dingy apartment in New Orleans. Back when…

* * *

The guests left. The door was closed.

"Whew, I'm exhausted," Marguerite said. "Didn't you have a good time, Tubby?" she asked as if the answer were important. "I've just met them, but they all seem like such really fantastic people. And just maybe they can be our new friends, friends just for the two of us."

"All great. All good," Tubby said, giving her hair a stroke. "Here, I'll help you clean up."

9

"No," Marguerite said. "Let's do that later. Right now I'd just like to take a shower. Then maybe, you know…" She gave him a gentle poke in the ribs.

He smiled and nodded. Marguerite affected a blush and danced away to the master bedroom.

Tubby watched her go, then remembered his empty glass. He went to the kitchen for another refill and took it back to the balcony. Where, in the glow of the descending sun, it was perfect. Where he closed his eyes, and remembered.

II

As a kid, Tubby had always imagined that he might be a crop duster, spraying Clearpath, Clincher and PropiMax in toxic clouds over the rice fields back home in Bunkie. But a high school wrestling trip to New Orleans changed his perspective profoundly. With the team's chaperone, their youth minister, leading the way, they took a walking tour down Bourbon Street. The warm springtime air was rich with the aroma of mystery and (he later learned) pot. Long-haired kids about his age confronted his group, and everyone else who chanced by, hawking The NOLA Express. It was a smudgy paper with an obscene cover that sold for a quarter a copy. The street people also sold cool buttons protesting the war in Vietnam, each for a dime. Some of these vendors seemed earnestly businesslike, but others appeared to be hippies. Tubby had heard about hippies, but these were the first he had ever seen. The girls had on face paint and weren't wearing bras.

Lining the uneven sidewalk littered with plastic cups and fried chicken parts were older men with skinny black ties and shirt sleeves rolled tightly around their biceps, who swung open the strip club doors and yelled, "All Naked! Nothing Hidden!" The young boys got brief glimpses of the dancing beauties inside. They elbowed each other and pointed, gawking in awe.

The wrestling team's chaperone was also brand new to this

scene, but it quickly registered with him as—Horror! He slammed it into reverse and hustled his charges back to Canal Street, onto a streetcar, and uptown to their dormitory. By then, however, the damage had been done. Tubby had bitten the apple of the knowledge of good and evil, and he was no longer satisfied with his previous rural and upright teenage life. He wanted more, lots more.

As soon as he got back to Bunkie he tackled his studies with a new purpose. College was his goal. His parents noticed the change, and were impressed. While still doing his hundred push-ups before school and staying after class for sports, he actually started to do his homework. He even turned on the TV news at night and began discussing things—the oil crisis and the creation of the Environmental Protection Agency, for instance, and he would also volunteer to present his arguments in class—like we ought to invade Saudi Arabia and take all the oil we want.

The Assistant Warden at Angola State Penitentiary was the graduation speaker. He urged the students to keep Christ in everything they did. Then Tubby was off to college. At the church school in Mississippi, favored by his parents, he had the good fortune to room with a rugged boy from Louisiana who became a lifelong friend, Raisin Partlow. In short order, however, Tubby set his sights on Tulane University. His father had gone there.

The young student bought a ticket on a Trailways bus from Jackson to New Orleans to explore the possibility of transferring, a venture financed by his father. Tubby was supposed to be gone only a couple of days, and arrangements were made for him to bunk in a Tulane dorm. But when Tubby got off the bus, he slung his canvas knapsack over his shoulder and immediately asked directions to the French Quarter.

Walking down the hot city streets, he kept his eyes on the

tops of the buildings. A few months earlier, a man had climbed to the roof of the Howard Johnson's and made national news by shooting at people on the sidewalks below, ultimately wounding or killing twenty-two, five of them policemen. The shooter's motive was to avenge racist oppression by killing whites.

The young traveler with his pinstriped shirt and pressed chinos managed to get to Bourbon Street safely. Even in the middle of the afternoon it was just as funky and exotic as he remembered it from his brief visit with the wrestling team. Ambling along the sidewalk, he encountered an endless supply of interesting people. He paused to study some advertisements for a naked stripper tacked on the side of a bar and happened to come to the attention of a derelict. The ragged man had a cane and a patch over one eye and he begged the teenager for some change. Something about the pathos and worldliness expressed by the man's good eye, yellow-streaked and red-rimmed though it was, touched Tubby's heart, and he extracted the wallet in which he kept a quarter nestled between a pair of twenty-dollar bills his father had supplied for this trip.

An urchin sprinted out of the crowd and plucked the wallet out of Tubby's hand as neatly as a lizard zaps a passing fly. The skinny thief rocketed around the corner, with Tubby yelling after him, and he was gone. Incredulous at this sudden change in fortune, Tubby turned to confront the panhandler, but he too had disappeared.

* * *

Sitting on the balcony in Naples, Tubby could still remember the awful lonesomeness of that moment. The French Quarter, so full of promise, enlightenment and fun a moment before, had suddenly turned dark and forbidding. Tubby realized that he had no money, and no ID, and he was miles from hearth and home. He was adrift in a dangerous and very big city.

The isolated teenager was comforted over this enormous loss by one of the newspaper peddlers who had seen this crime go down. The observer was a burly guy, like Tubby, and had the scraggly beginnings of a red beard. The hair on his head was as long and disheveled as a Viking's.

"I'm supposed to interview at Tulane tomorrow," Tubby moaned to the universe. He was bereft. He asked the paper seller if he could borrow a dime to call his dad.

"Not too sure about that," the big man said. He introduced himself as Dan Haywood. Tubby said, call me "Streak," a nickname he had gotten on the wrestling team. "I'm going to the cops," he insisted with determination.

"I don't advise it," the peddler said. A nearby mounted policeman was already looking them over and smacking his nightstick into his palm.

Dan walked off and Tubby followed, too disconsolate to think of a better option.

Blocks away, on a balcony at the top of a rickety staircase, they joined a group of young people hanging out over a flowered, brick-walled courtyard, wreathed in smoke. Inside the apartment two girls were making steaming pots of lentils and carrots. All of the inhabitants, Tubby's new friends, embraced him like a brother.

He learned about each one's situation.

There was a draft dodger.

A draft counselor.

A writing instructor at a Catholic university.

A business major at UNO.

An illegal from Greece.

A woman who had been arrested with Avery Alexander when he had been dragged up the steps at City hall.

A pot smoker.

A country-music enthusiast who thought the rebel South would rise again.

Girls with unbuttoned shirts.

A parrot.

Tubby explained that he was a college wrestler, and they all laughed in disbelief.

The group was talking over the oppressiveness of New Orleans and the "shootout at Desire," where police tanks had been deployed against the Black Panthers. But most of all, they talked about the latest news of the war, all of which dismayed and outraged them. There was supposed to be a peace accord, but the fighting continued, and now we were bombing Cambodia, providing more fuel for their daily demonstrations against the unspeakable conflict.

Tubby passed a very insightful evening with them. He slept well, his head on a young lady's lap, and left early the next morning for his college interview. He clutched a handful of change provided by one of the women who cared little about material things. The interview went well. At its conclusion, he took the streetcar back downtown to grab his pack and figure out his next move. But as soon as he disembarked on Canal Street, he was surprised to encounter his new companions, who were demonstrating on the neutral ground.

* * *

Now, almost 40 years later, Tubby was amazed to recall how he had made friends so quickly. He wished he could have such ease again, such friends again. They all believed in a better future. The old order (the old people) would die out soon enough.

"I didn't die out," Tubby said, again forgetting that he was by himself on a breezy balcony over the Gulf.

The sun was setting once more, as it did every day, in a blaze of exotic colors, primary orange and azure streaks shooting across the edge of the flat blue sea.

Marguerite called to him, "Tubby, don't you want to come inside and relax?"

Tubby closed his eyes and drifted back to that afternoon on the neutral ground.

III

Around the demonstrators, the sidewalks were full of people. Tubby had to clear a path through them to reach his group. The protesters were waving signs, like "END THE WAR!"

"What's up?" he asked.

"The Secretary of State in town to make a speech at the World Trade Center," one of the protestors yelled.

Pedestrians on Canal Street hustled about their business. Ladies shopping in flowery hats and white gloves were clustered outside the big department stores. Businessmen in seersucker suits and wingtips lit cigars as they walked and talked deals.

The demonstrators attracted more than a few stares because they were loud, but no one in the noontime crowd was particularly threatening. Most of the protestors were serious-looking short-haired kids. Only a couple wore colorful, grubby attire, cowboy boots and torn jeans, with fringed vests covered with protest buttons. But they made the populace aware of the intensity of their feeling and purpose. They had rallied around what they called the White Supremacy Monument, a tribute to the overthrow of black Reconstruction rule, which commanded the middle of the wide neutral ground.

Tubby's impressions of this day had been made a little opaque by the passage of time, but he did remember a United Cab driver who shook his fist out the window and called them

Pinkos. A Lucky Dog vendor pushed his cart through the protest, trying to get into the French Quarter. Tubby certainly recalled being told to take note of the three muscular men, Beatle haircuts and pressed jeans, standing across the street in front of a sprawling concrete municipal building made in the shape of a flattened white mushroom. They were joking among themselves, trying to look hip.

"Cops?" he asked.

"Chief Giarrusso's finest," he was told.

A block away, uniformed policemen abruptly marched into the intersection and stopped traffic to make way for a caravan of black limousines.

"That must be Kissinger!" a protester cried.

The street blockade set off a din of blaring car horns. Three blocks full of trapped vehicles maneuvered this way and that trying to get across the neutral ground on which the demonstrators stood so that they could make U-turns.

The protesters continued waving their signs and yelling for attention, but the general mayhem drowned them out. Tubby could recall the deafening uproar of the peace chants, the jeers, the sirens and horns, all the car exhaust, the heat.

Maybe that's why he didn't notice the car full of hecklers idling alongside them until one of them hurled a tomato. It spattered on one of the kid's sign and dribbled onto his new faded madras shirt.

"Hey, what!" the protester objected and shot a bird at his assailant, a person who was only a blur in the back seat.

"Assholes!" the demonstrator's girlfriend screamed, and more projectiles came out of the car.

"Communist bastards!" someone shouted.

Suddenly there was a bright flash and a pop from the back of the car.

The boy dropped his sign and looked down at his chest in

dismay. Blood was bubbling out, a red ribbon following the buttons of his neat shirt, dripping over his belt. His knees buckled.

Everyone was screaming. The car lurched forward and bucked the curb. It swerved across the streetcar tracks, scattering people, and blasted away from the scene on Canal Street.

Tubby dropped to the pavement and tried to stuff his own shirttails into the boy's wound. As bystanders fled, the three undercover cops ran between cars and excitedly inspected the victim. The wounded boy squinted at the relentless sun and closed his eyes.

A new crowd formed, trying to see what had happened.

Tubby's attempts to staunch the flow of blood failed miserably. His hands were covered with it. He looked up at the cops helplessly.

"Poor Parker!" one of the girls wailed.

It seemed to take a long time, but an ambulance finally sirened its way through traffic. It carried the pale demonstrator and two of the cops away and left everyone else milling about on the curb, except for one of the young women whom the police pushed to the sidewalk and arrested for trying to claw her way into the ambulance. The other cop dragged her around the corner.

Tubby and Dan ran the dozen blocks to Charity Hospital while the remnants of the demonstrators dispersed, presumably in search of sympathetic doctors and the free lawyer the street people used. When Tubby and Dan eventually found the Emergency Room, they were told to sit in the Pine-Sol-smelling waiting area with the gasping sick people and all the crying kids with broken arms. Finally they were called up to the desk by a white-bonneted nurse who informed them that their friend was dead.

"Did he have any family?" the nurse asked.

Tubby and Dan looked at each other sadly.

IV

Tubby most often avoided thinking about the human condition. He had not been too sure about his own for months. He now found himself in Naples soaking up the sunset, and he didn't have a clue what he was doing here. Once upon a time his aim had been true. Turn that sundial back ten or fifteen years, and he had known exactly what he was doing.

In those days he was a quick-thinking New Orleans lawyer on the make, and he was succeeding at it. He had scored big in the Pan Am airplane disaster and opened his expansive and expensive office on the 43rd floor of the Place Palais Building in downtown New Orleans, with its custom millwork and a splendid conference table. He had a slick and aggressive partner in Reggie Turntide, who could bring in rich clients. And he was married to his redheaded college sweetheart, Mattie Berkenbaum. They had an excellent family, consisting of three happy little girls.

Then it all started to unpeel, one layer at a time. Inexplicably, Mattie announced that she was moving out to find more space for herself. Actually, it was Tubby who ended up moving. Mattie got the nice house on State Street and most of the time she got the kids. Then his partner Reggie disappeared. Dan Haywood reemerged briefly in his life but soon was senselessly, terribly, shot dead during the great Mardi Gras flood. Tubby distractedly ran his fingers through his blond hair for another minute and soaked up the sun.

After that, all the violence and corruption in New Orleans began to shove aside, in his mind, the city's alluring beauty, color and pageantry. Tubby began to sense the existence of a criminal web, woven by a toxic spider, a truly evil presence, a crime czar. So obsessed with this evil force did Tubby become that he could almost smell it. The quest to find the Czar took him deeply into the city's underworld and now, even with the brutal elimination of the high and mighty Sheriff Mulé, he couldn't say for certain that the menace had been exterminated.

Then came Katrina, the big one, that turned the world as he knew it upside down. He still couldn't fathom how it had happened, but the storm had changed everything. Along with the mountains of old refrigerators, water heaters, wet sheetrock and backyard junk hauled away by the government went the assuredness that the carefree city would always be the same: that there would always be a Schwegmanns; that the Nevilles would always play "Hey Pocky Way"; that Ninth Warders would always fill the nosebleed seats in the Dome; that sleepy sunny days would always sashay along, very sweetly, in four-four time.

And paradoxically, as a result of all that loss and destruction, Tubby found his love for the city returning.

So what the heck was he doing in Florida, the land of the Everglades and orange juice fudge? He was here with his rich girlfriend, of course, though she was a bit larcenous. He was on the rebound, or resurface. His last love, Hope, with whom he had survived Katrina, had succumbed to a long illness that had too quickly consumed her completely. In all candor, it was probably too early for him to be dating ladies, but Tubby had been down in the dumps and wanted cheering up. And he was not a monk.

Back in Louisiana, his daughters were all doing just fine in his opinion. Debbie, his oldest, still married, was the vice-president of a start-up investment company, and had a 12-year-old basketball player at Newman named Arnie, but called "Bat." Christine, who had had a miserable time during Hurricane Katrina, was now a paleontologist at LSU and lived with a girlfriend. Collette, the youngest, had never strayed far from home. She was currently on her third fiancé, a rap performer who claimed to be from the Dry Tortugas. All in all, just fine. They possibly didn't need him, hard as that was to believe. But he found that he was starting to miss them and the exuberance of the city.

New Orleans, when you stepped back and looked at it, was also doing really great. All cleaned up. Bursting with young entrepreneurs, movie trailers blocking every street. Here by the beaches of Florida he was starting to know what it means to miss New Orleans.

"I shouldn't be sitting here on my butt. I don't deserve this paradise," he lectured himself. "I should be headed home. But first let me go see what Marguerite has on her mind."

V

A few days after the shooting on Canal Street, in a cramped downtown office with nothing on the walls, the first order of business was to discuss the demonstrator they had killed.

Mostly the young men conducted their meetings in English but it was definitely *bueno* to chime in with the occasional Spanish epithet or significant old saying. The meetings stuck to a strict agenda, which was always laid out by their Leader, whose father had been the Leader before him. The members were serious about the program because their mission was extremely serious. They avoided using each other's real names at these meetings. Big Brother could be watching. No doubt about it.

Individual assignments were handed out at their gatherings and if expenses were expected, the Leader provided the details. The Recorder kept track of it all, and Security kept them all safe. The Night Watchman saw to the purity of their ideology and the delivery of their message.

Much of what the youth group did was secretive, naturally, but behind them were even more hidden figures, known as the "Committee." It was the source of most of their funds. The youth group members knew who some of the men on the Committee were because those old warriors occasionally appeared before the group to give inspirational talks. One of the Committee was "Senior," and another was known as the "Judge." No full names, please, but of course the members knew who they were. These giants were all important public figures.

The boys venerated them. After all, they had killed Kennedy, yes? And gotten away with it. Anyway, that was what the whisperers said. To a man, both young and old, they were steadfast and true to their cause, which was to "Free Cuba" and "Halt the March of Socialism."

Almost all of these boys, there were no girls, had parents who had fled the island. Their property had been stolen by the Communists. Three of the youths had fathers, or uncles, who had sailed into the Bay of Pigs with Ricardo Duque and who had been betrayed there by JFK. These soldiers, whether they were alive or dead, were like gods.

"Shooting deviants is a good thing," the Leader said. "That was a good clean kill."

"Was that in the escalation plan?" his Second-in-Command asked. "Was that what we meant by taking the ball to the..."

"The scum." Another boy, the Recorder, finished his sentence.

"Is anyone pointing a finger at us?" the Leader asked. "Should we have any fear of an investigation?"

"No. None whatsoever," came the deep voice of Security, the one who was in the Young Police League. "They're going through the motions, but no one identified your car or the license plate."

"That's what I hear, too," the Night Watchman agreed.

"Then we've had good luck," the Leader said.

"No. It was good execution," Security replied.

"Lord's will," the Night Watchman muttered.

"Who is available to run the mimeograph machine tonight?" the Leader asked.

Three hands went up.

"I've got to take my mother to church," the Vice-President explained.

VI

After the shooting on Canal Street, Tubby lost his way for a while. He never did tell his father or his friends back home what he had seen. Witnessing the death of the boy he knew only as "Parker," however, dramatically altered his intention of enlisting in the Marines. Somehow the mindless violence he had witnessed connected in his mind with the unending daily tragedies overseas, which were also featured stories on the 6 o'clock news.

Unaware that his recruit had become troubled, the Tulane counselor, true to his word, got Tubby into the university.

The French Quarter spirits he had known so briefly scattered to the winds. He got a postcard from Dan explaining that he was enlisting in the National Guard to "subvert from within." He got into the Guard based on a recommendation from his state representative in Canton, Mississippi. One of the girls moved off to the Blue Ridge Mountains where life was simple and pure. His friend Raisin Partlow stayed in touch. He dropped out of his Mississippi college and was immediately drafted and sent to Vietnam. In his Tulane dorm Tubby received regular letters from Raisin, who was fixing helicopters near Danang in Vietnam. The consistent theme, repeated over and over, was "Don't the fuck even think about coming over here, whatever you do!"

But Tubby, the small town boy, thought he probably should go over there. He was supposed to join the ROTC as part of his school financial package but, wouldn't you know it, someone burned the Tulane ROTC building down the night the Chicago 7 came to town. One problem solved.

School started going poorly. He became involved with a sophomore English major. In the ways of the time, what initially attracted him was that she had breasts like ripe cantaloupes, a comparison that came easily to him, having grown up on a farm. She was, however, very depressed as a general rule, not about the war or anything like that, but about her relationship with her father, her mother, her sisters. She would drink wine, then come over to Tubby's room and cry. This had a chilling effect on his libido, which in turn depressed him, too. So he broke it off.

Events began to spin faster and faster. Dan was expelled from the Guard as an undesirable, and then went "undercover," he said, to organize for some union. Most of the Tulane undergraduate students began to seem preppy beyond belief, or were too far into drugs to appeal to Tubby. Spirits low, he gave vent to an irrational burst of anger at a teacher about some interpretation of Chaucer's Canterbury Tales. The professor, feeling physically intimidated, kicked him out of class. In retaliation Tubby quit school.

In a split second he was drafted. Right before his induction ceremony, Raisin came home.

"What the fuck did I tell you, man? Don't go there!" he insisted over Heinekens at Fat Harry's. Beer had become legal for 18-year-olds.

"Of course I'm going," Tubby said angrily. "What else am I supposed to do?"

Two weeks after he crossed the line, leaving aimless civilian life behind, the peace accord went out the window, and the

National Liberation Army raced south. In the middle of his basic training at Fort Polk, Saigon fell.

Tubby never left the country. In fact, he never left New Jersey. Due to his size he spent what was left of his two years of national service as a Military Police trainee. As an MP, he guarded the tarmac at Fort Dix and got to salute planeloads of men, those upright and those laid flat, coming home from various parts of the globe. In his country's service he also competed on the Army's wrestling team, and he got every muscle in his body bruised and torn by far better athletes than the blond boy from Louisiana. After beating the crap out of him they gave him the name "Tubby". He was cool with that. They called themselves much worse things. Then he was discharged.

Raisin, Dan Haywood, and Tubby all came home with at least one thing in common. All three now knew there was definitely one thing that they never wanted to do again. Be in the Army. A noble calling, but…

Tubby's Greyhound took him back to his hometown of Bunkie. A month later he was readmitted to Tulane. Only this time around his course in life was straight. With his muscles and bones mending, and his tuition paid by the government, Tubby began to see the point of getting educated. He met another English major named Mattie, and they started sleeping over at each other's apartments. Tubby made the grades and graduated. Then he went to law school, and the rest, as they say, is history.

VII

The boy who couldn't work the mimeograph machine for the anti-socialist youth group didn't take his mother to church. That was just an excuse. Instead he went home and crawled into bed where he stayed for two entire days. He told his mother he was tired, and she made him pay the price. She served him *sopa de pollo* and rubbed hot chili powder on his chest. She fed him *nonni fruit* and massaged VapoRub into his feet.

He had not been in the car that day, the day when they shot the war protester, and he hadn't even known it had happened until he went to the meeting. The matter-of-fact way it was reported to the group horrified him.

"You're missing your classes," his mother prodded him. "Here, have some soup…"

Yes, he was missing classes. He was supposed to be carrying a full load at the University of New Orleans, and he was blowing it. Why had he ever gotten involved with this group? They were totally *loco*.

But of course he knew why he went to those meetings. His father spent all of his time listening to Cuban and Miami radio on the shortwave. Dad was so embittered by the revolution that he had barely been able to work for fifteen years.

"Our shoe store is sitting right there, right where we left it," he told his son. "It was my father's store. It was my store. I have the keys, and we could walk right in tomorrow. It is the place where you were born. It is yours now, Son, just as soon as we go back."

But the boy had his doubts. He couldn't remember anything much about Cuba, except for grainy mental photographs of a pink stucco house shrouded by green banana trees. And he remembered a fearsome red parrot who followed him from room to room defecating. His mother had given him birthday parties and invited lots of friends, but he wasn't positive that they had ever happened in Cuba. Maybe it was later, in Miami or later still in New Orleans. She gave him parties like that to this day.

His father didn't seem to be in any of these mental pictures. Maybe it was because his father was actually or figuratively always working in that damn store. Now Pop stayed home all the time and was eternally sad. He wasn't a lot of help when it came to planning his son's future.

The boy saw a career for himself in banking, or in advertising maybe. His father just wanted the family to go back to Cuba and sell shoes.

The boy's girlfriend dropped by on the third day.

"What's the matter with you?" she asked.

"I'm very tired and sick," he said.

She checked to be sure the mom wasn't looking and then gave him a quick kiss on the lips and a firm squeeze on his crotch through his jeans.

"Get up and go to school," she said. So he did.

He caught the bus out to the lakefront the next morning and returned to class, but it wasn't really over. The group had killed someone. The frightened student looked for FBI men in the shadows of every oak tree.

It was an unspeakable relief, as the days went by, to find no mention whatsoever of this crime in the newspapers. No TV. No nothing. None of his fellow conspirators reported anything that would concern any of them.

Yet over the course of a month he had lost eleven pounds worrying.

In time, however, the event faded into the past. In spite of this, he stopped going to the meetings. He explained to the group that his mother needed help around the house, since his father was always so sad. They bought that. By plodding through every day and applying himself, he eventually got his degree and went out in search of a career. Except at family gatherings, Cuba and international socialism rarely crossed his mind.

But as life went on there was still that little, deep, scared place in his head.

VIII

It was on the flight back from Florida to New Orleans that Tubby again started thinking about that murder. He wasn't sure why, since forty years had passed. Maybe it was the more recent senseless killing of the young man, Trayvon Martin, but, for whatever reason, he couldn't get it out of his head. He wondered whether anything had ever been done about it. He knew that he had never been questioned by the police.

In a strange way, his grown-up personality had been shaped by that bullet. Not all of his personality, of course. Before that had been a hazy stretch of undemanding days in Bunkie, and after that there had been the army, graduate school, a family, clients by the hundreds, all with stories to tell, lost loves, tragedies, and mysteries galore.

But with that gunshot had come a glimpse into the terrible and final way the world could treat people, and the way it would keep right on treating people if nobody stepped in.

Tubby could never claim that he had spent a career championing the cause of the downtrodden. Like most lawyers, of course, he had saved his share of widows, orphans and fools from tragic fates, but the fact was that he had charged what the market would bear and made a pretty good living at it. He appreciated being one of the chosen few—the ones who could go past the swinging courtroom gates and approach the bench.

He got to knock back a big heap of crawfish with a judge now and then. Not everybody could do that. But he had always been skeptical of the system itself, even though he was a part of it. It was troubling at this time of his life to ask what he was doing with that exceptional power. What of significance, that is?

Such heavy thoughts bothered Tubby. They didn't bother him so much for their content but just because he didn't like to have to deal with heavy thoughts. Somehow, however, Naples' detached beauty had brought them up against his will and now he was stuck with thinking them through.

The warm embrace of New Orleans' humidity hit him as soon as he walked out of the terminal and flagged a cab. It was late in the afternoon, and the sun was in full command of the heavens. The air conditioner in the cab wasn't working.

"Sorry, man," the driver apologized. "It sure ain't no picnic driving this old heap."

In the back seat Tubby tried to remain absolutely motionless, despite banging against the door as they bounced down New Orleans' corrugated streets. The heat caressed him through the opened windows. His heavy thoughts kept him company all the way down the Earhart Expressway.

"Been raining any?" he asked the cabdriver miserably.

"Not since July. But no hurricanes yet," he was told.

What sustained the passage was the vision of his shady house Uptown. When the cab finally got there and crunched to the curb, Tubby had his wallet ready. He paid the fare plus a tip, got his bag from the trunk, and inhaled deeply. There it was—the familiar and restorative smell of gardenias and soggy grass, coffee brewing and very close, the Mississippi River.

The house within was just as he'd left it two weeks before. He locked the front door and pushed down the thermostat, which made the air conditioner shudder on. Then he found himself a bottle of bourbon in the kitchen and fixed himself a big icy drink.

Home at last!

He sat on a kitchen stool to enjoy the solitude and quiet, looking out the window at his overgrown backyard full of red azaleas in full bloom. Why had he ever left?

He let his mind drift.

Parker, who the hell was he? What kind of person could he have become if he had lived? But really, who cared about him? Tubby was surprised that he did. What the hell was ever done about that murder?

IX

He was still on his first cup of Community coffee in the morning when the phone in his jeans started to vibrate.

"Hey, Man, are you back in New Orleans?" It was Raisin.

"Yeah. I just got in last night. How'd you know?"

"Because you called me last night and left a message? You don't remember?"

"Uh…" No, he didn't. Must have been somewhere between the third and fourth belt. It had taken quite a lot to put himself to sleep, after all that strenuous travel from Florida. All those heavy memories. He worried about whom else he might have called.

"You asked if I wanted to have lunch today," Raisin continued. "I was out with Sadie at the Maple Leaf listening to Joe Krown and never heard the phone ring. But the answer is yes."

Tubby had to dig deep to remember who Sadie was. He had been full of energy a moment ago but now, reminded that he had over-indulged the night before, he felt disoriented. Oh yeah, she was some sort of engineer at Shell, recently relocated to New Orleans from Holland. Raisin had met her at the tennis club and managed to make a good impression, as he usually did when wearing whites.

"Good. We'll meet. I'm going to the office this morning

and see if I still have a law practice. That probably won't take very long. Where do you want to go?"

"How about out in the Bywater?" You remember Janie, the bartender at Grits? I think I may have a client for you."

Which is how they ended up at Monkey Business on St. Claude Avenue, way across the tracks. It was in one of the older parts of town, a neighborhood of shotguns hugging the Mississippi River levee, full of roughnecks, gospel-singing grannies, longshoremen, mamas in green spandex at the bus stops, po-boy shops and lots of fried chicken, noodle, and beer joints. And lately, artists, urban planners, filmmakers, and start-up entrepreneurs had moved in, creating the newest outer fringe of hip culture in New Orleans.

Tubby's detour to the office was uneventful. Cherrylynn, his long-time secretary, had kept up with the phone and emails for the past two weeks with her usual competence. Quite honestly, Tubby hadn't really been working his law practice for a couple of years, so her job wasn't full-time-interesting nowadays. In fact, he was considering bringing in a young lawyer to keep her occupied and to handle the business that Tubby fancied he could generate if he really put his mind to it. In the interim Cherrylynn had been taking afternoon classes at Loyola University studying philosophy, politics, and economics. Only thirty-two more credits to a college degree.

He had also picked a very good time to go on a Florida vacation. To say that August was a slow time at the courthouse would be an insult to stoned sloths. There were summer days when you couldn't find a member of the judiciary anywhere in the building, not even at their normal midday rendezvous presiding over raw oysters and Trout Meuniere at Mandina's.

Monkey Business, the bar, encroached on the sidewalk and was almost in the street. Its warped cypress siding was painted white with a faded advertisement for Regal Beer, a defunct brand, and it even boasted a sprayed-on "X" in a circle, the red mark left by Katrina's first responders indicating the number of bodies and abandoned pets found within.

"This is a classic joint," Tubby said appreciatively as he got out of the car. "Do they actually serve lunch?"

"Good fried shrimp," Raisin replied, climbing out from behind the wheel of the used red Miata his girlfriend had picked up for him. Tubby stretched mightily, afraid he might have thrown his back out just getting into the damned thing.

Coming in from the blazing sun it was dark in the bar. When his eyes adjusted Tubby beheld a comfortably familiar layout. A long bar trailed off into a back room fitted with a stage, a handful of tables. A few patrons sat at the bar or at tables, concentrating on their beers and their private conversations.

Bustling toward these arrivals came a large brassy woman wearing an x-tra large lumberjack shirt, a dirty white Stetson hat, and flip flops.

"Here they are, the old sexy dudes!" she brayed, and gave them each a crushing hug. Tubby hadn't seen Janie for years, since way before the hurricane. Those intervening years of two packs a day had made her voice even huskier. The dimness of her professional environment had made her skin even whiter. Her merry face was crisscrossed with tiny pink veins. The beer had made her even stouter. He wouldn't want to arm-wrestle her.

"It's so good to see you again, Tubby," she rejoiced.

"What about me?" Raisin asked.

"You, too, but I already seen you last week. Here it is. My new place!" She swept it all up in the sails of her arms. "It ain't much, but we're doing all right. Come on. Pick a table and get a seat."

They settled in, scratching their chairs along the wooden floor.

"Jack!" she yelled. "Bring us all a drink. I'm going to have one, too." She winked at Tubby. "This is a reunion, right, darlin'?"

The drinks came quickly. Jack was a young guy with a plaid shirt and a trim beard who looked like he had just flown in from Portland. He was in shape. A capable bouncer, Tubby speculated.

"So, what's been going on with you, my love?" Janie asked loudly. "Raisin tells me you're still the best lawyer in town."

Tubby went over it – how he had fared in the hurricane, what he had been doing since, how his kids had grown up. "I had a bar of my own, too," he told her. "Mike's, down in the Irish Channel."

"I heard about that," Janie said. "Sorry I never made it over. You don't still own it?"

"Yes, he does," Raisin put in.

"No, I don't. I sold it to Pinky Laparouse two years ago."

"You've got a mortgage on it," Raisin insisted.

"I do," Tubby admitted. "But, Janie, how did you end up on this side of the city?"

"You remember Grits," she began. Of course. Their old Uptown watering hole, where Janie had listened patiently to all sorts of troubles while mixing up passable Old Fashioneds. The storm closed it down for a while, and it also sent Janie fleeing for higher ground. She had bounced around for a couple of years taking care of her mother. Within the community of dispossessed imbibers she had met and married Bud Caragliano, ten years her senior, so she claimed.

"Ever meet Bud?" she asked. Raisin and Tubby shook their heads.

"He was a good guy, as long as he was drinking," Janie said.

"Well, anyway he used to own this little place. It took about three feet of water in Katrina. Then he got stage-four lung cancer and died. But he left this bar to me. I put together a few bucks and we got it all cleaned up. It was just a dive at first. But then the neighborhood changed."

"Downhill?" Tubby asked.

"Hell, no!" she bawled out. "It's a friggin' gold mine now. This crowd you see here…" she waved at the half-a-dozen guys wearing grimy T-shirts and tool belts, "…they clear out by five, and later on tonight I get an unbelievable number of kids. They pack this joint, baby!"

"Hmmm." Tubby tried to imagine that. The bar did have a cool atmosphere. It was dark. There was a neon Dixie Beer sign on the wall. The TV over the bar was tuned to a baseball game, and the sound was turned off. He thought he saw grass growing out of the floor over by the jukebox. Certainly traditional.

"Let me get you some lunch," Janie offered. "How about a shrimp po-boy? We can make up other things if you'd rather. We got an eggplant mozzarella wrap, gluten free."

"What's gluten?"

"Yeah, well, I don't know. But I recommend the shrimp. It's our cook's specialty."

"You even have a cook?" Tubby was impressed.

"My daughter Sophia. I'll introduce you."

Jack brought another round. Janie didn't get down to business until the food arrived, mountains of golden crisp shrimp piled on French bread and spilling out of the plates. Pickles, tomatoes, Crystal hot sauce. As a lagniappe, the cook had sent each of them a bowl of rich brown steamy chicken and sausage gumbo.

"What's this in the gumbo? Potato salad?" Tubby exclaimed. Indeed the soup had been ladled over the homespun alternative to white rice. "It smells delicious," he said, enraptured. It created the perfect moment to pitch a lawyer.

"I'm having trouble with the city," Janie explained. "They don't like me having live music here every night."

"Why not?" Tubby asked, enjoying a loose shrimp. "What kind of music do you put on?" Tubby was having a hard time getting his hands around his sandwich, so he speared three errant shrimp with his fork and popped them into his mouth.

"All kinds of music," Janie said. "We had Paul Sanchez here. And Gal Holiday. We had the Luminescent Lizards. We get folk stuff. We get Indie. We got soft and we got loud. But that's the problem."

"Loud?" Tubby repeated. He anticipated what was coming.

"Yes, indeed. Loud! Which has got some of the neighbors upset. Worse than that, it's got me dealing with the zoning flunkies and the quality of life cops. It ain't pretty."

"They want you to turn it down?"

"They want me to turn it off! And guess what, they want to jerk my license because they say St. Claude ain't zoned for bars and music."

"You're kidding me." Tubby was incredulous. To his left Raisin glared and shook his head at such municipal stupidity. "What are we here?" Tubby continued. "The Ninth Ward? The birthplace of the brass band, the jazz funeral and the second line? The cradle of New Orleans music culture. The womb of…"

"He's getting it," Raisin interrupted.

"I know, it doesn't make sense," Janie said sadly. "But now you know my problem. And this comes when for the first time in my life I'm making lots of money."

A paying client? Tubby sat back in his rickety chair and cleared his mind. He brushed the crumbs off his chest. "Tell me all about it," he said.

* * *

There had been a time when Tubby had been much better connected to the police force. He had been pals with Homicide Detective Fox Lane, a five-foot-ten inch, 105 pound, marathon-running dedicated cop. About the time of Katrina, however, she had taken a bullet in the chest in the line of duty, accepted her pension, and now was chief security officer at Alluvial Bank. Chasing white-collar embezzlers and money launderers was a lot safer than chasing Seventh Ward narco gangs.

So he called up his own private investigator, Sanré Fueres, who called himself Flowers. He was still in his prime, still single, and was still going down dark alleys.

"You been out of town?" Flowers asked.

"I was down in Florida for a couple of weeks working on my tan."

"With Marguerite?"

"How'd you know that?"

"Right."

"I need a little help with New Orleans finest. Have you ever heard of something called a quality of life officer?"

"Sure. I don't think I know any of them, but those are the guys who check out convenience stores selling vodka to minors, loud music, vacation rentals by owner, things like that."

"Really? Well it's loud music I'm concerned with. Out on St. Claude Avenue in the Ninth Ward."

"On this side of the Industrial Canal?"

"Exactly." The other side of the Canal was a flood-ravaged wasteland dotted with new experimental houses financed by Brad Pitt. Maybe it would be the next target for hip rejuvenation, depending on how you read the cards. Today's leaky-roofed and abandoned fixer-upper was tomorrow's organic juice bar or sexy clothing boutique.

"You're going to be in the Fifth Police District. I don't actually know any cops over there. No, wait, I know about one guy. He's being punished for something and got transferred out there. You want to talk to him? Or do you want me to?"

"Why don't you call him and see if he'll talk to me? I'd like to get to know some of the police working in that area."

"Okay. I'll take a shot and get back to you."

"Thanks." Knowing Flowers, that would take about twenty minutes.

It took fifteen.

"Guy's name is Officer Ireanous Babineaux."

"Jesus, that's quite a name. What do they call him?"

"Officer Ireanous Babineaux."

"Fine."

"I got his cell number. We swapped texts. He's willing to meet you for coffee and a doughnut if you like tomorrow morning at Elizabeth's Restaurant on Gallier Street."

"I'll have to look that one up."

"It's by the river. He says eight o'clock."

"Thanks. I'll be there."

* * *

That frightened, scared place was buried far down in the young man's mind. Deep, but always there. Even when he wasn't so young anymore it was still there. His proximity to the shooting affected him in ways he didn't fully know about. He never got married, for instance, possibly fretful of being too candid with another living soul.

Steady jobs held no allure, though with a business background and all the engineering courses he'd taken he was certainly qualified for one. He took no interest whatsoever in politics, or in the causes his parents espoused, and he kept an extremely tight circle of friends. Not that he liked solitude, because he didn't. But instead of community engagement he took to the horses.

The Fairgrounds Race Track was the best place in the whole world to him. The Racing Form meant more than the chemist's periodic table, the broker's NASDAQ index, the entertainer's score or the gambler's dice. He worshipped the odds calculator on his iPhone app, and he was working out ways to improve it—twists he could patent or copyright, ideas he could sell for a buck. His laboratory was the air-conditioned grandstand, smelling vaguely of hot dogs, mustard and hay, where he could be found every race day between Thanksgiving and Mardi Gras.

When Louisiana's racing season ended in the spring, he might take a girlfriend up north to party and bet at Belmont or Pimlico, or he might just kick back in his Lakeside townhouse, close the curtains and work his brain. Cutting-edge, youth-oriented, consumerism fascinated him. He was always conceiving new things to sell to that market. Not everything he conjured up about caffeinated vodka or spray-on pheromones was a winner, but enough were hits that he made money and could keep his life insulated from the oh-so boring, oh-so threatening world. He drove a Lexus. He got take-out swordfish tacos and ropa vieja whenever he felt like it. Or sushi, if he wanted to forget where he had come from.

X

Elizabeth's Restaurant was a very happening place, once you found it. Tubby went the slow route, not on purpose, but that's the way it turned out. He piloted his newest car, a black 1978 Camaro with the spoiler on the back, which got nine miles to the gallon, all the way through the French Quarter and its throng of tourists—hurrying along to Café du Monde for their beignets and café au lait. It was still an early hour, but this was when sugary days began. The visitors were serenaded by ships' horns, trolley bells and clanking train cars, none of which they had at eight a.m. in Chevy Chase.

As usual Tubby got lost as soon as he crossed Esplanade Avenue into the Faubourg Marigny. All of a sudden the streets angled off in crazy directions. No big deal to the local man. It was still only seven-forty-five. However, he was challenged and blocked. On Chartres Street, a Rock Star Waste Disposal truck idled in his path. The workers slammed gigantic plastic garbage cans over the curbs and gave each other commands in an unintelligible tongue. When he finally burst free, he found himself in a neighborhood he knew virtually nothing about.

But it wasn't hostile. Little girls wearing school uniforms were carrying their backpacks to class. Delivery trucks were dropping off bread and vegetables at the corner stores. There were lots of quaint restaurants and special shops, all closed at this hour but emitting people who rented the apartments upstairs and at this hour had to hustle to work. Such cool people, Tubby thought. Mostly young and looking healthy. Jeans and sneakers and flowery cotton prints and layers were the style. And here he was, still stuck in a suit and tie.

The scene took him back to his own street-people period. All 72 hours of it. These kids had energy, like he once had, and were undoubtedly more clear-headed than his youthful friends had been. They looked like they were headed somewhere to apply themselves and pick up a paycheck. He found a place to park in front of the abandoned Toledo Iron Works.

Opening the door of the café he almost got run over by a tall woman wearing a spotless white polo shirt and black slacks, both of which hugged her trim figure. She looked like a prep school gym teacher and had a phone pressed against her short brown hair. Tubby got an apologetic smile as she brushed past. She had no obvious lipstick. Her black eyes were spaced far apart.

The restaurant was full, and it was lucky that the police officer was already seated and noticed him, which wasn't hard. He was the big lawyer wearing a tie. The cop waved Tubby over. The décor was striking, walls covered with cryptic sayings like, "Don't Tread on Me," written in splashes of color, Dr. Bob's version of folk art in wooden frames outlined in bottle caps.

"Ireanous?" he inquired.

"Close enough," the cop said. His blue uniform shirt was crisply pressed, and his badge shone brightly on his broad chest. His skin, exposed above the neck, was nearly black. He wore a heavy mustache, but his head was shaved smooth. "Have a seat," he directed.

Tubby did. "Thanks for meeting me, Officer. I hope I can buy you some breakfast."

"Already ate, but I'll join you for another cup of coffee if you like. The Redneck Eggs are good."

Tubby shot him a glance to see if he meant something, but the ebony-toned policeman stared impassively back. "What's your name again?" he asked.

"Dubonnet."

"Rhymes with 'Make my day'?"

"That's it."

A waitress appeared, a dainty girl in a pink frock. Tubby pointed to the first special on the menu.

"So what's up?" Ireanous asked. "Your man Flowers didn't say much. 'Course I hardly know him."

"There's really not a whole lot to it. I represent the lady who owns the Monkey Business club over on St. Claude, and apparently she's run afoul of some local ordinances."

"Yeah? I know where that place is. They get some big crowds on weekends. But I've never heard about any trouble there." Ireanous paused to check his phone. "Of course, I haven't been in this precinct but a couple of weeks."

The waitress brought them both coffee and a plate of Eggs Elizabeth for Tubby. They appeared as a pair of perfect little poached eggs on French bread rounds, each with its dollop of golden creamy hollandaise, garnished with parsley and resting on a pea-green sheen of tarragon sauce, with yellow cheese grits on the side.

"Impressive," Babineaux commented.

"Absolutely," Tubby agreed, thinking that maybe the dish wasn't very macho looking. But it was tasty.

"I heard you just got transferred in," he said to the policeman.

"That's right," Ireanous said without expression. He didn't offer the details. His large eyes, starkly white against his skin, studied the lawyer carefully.

"You like it here?" Tubby asked.

"What the fuck is there to like about it?" the cop asked. "Drugs, guns, and kids who will shoot you just to prove their manhood. Every single person on the street has been to Parish Prison."

This was in stark contrast to Tubby's impression. "It doesn't look that bad to me, just driving around," he said, "but you make it sound pretty dismal."

Ireanous shrugged. "Whole city is like that," he added and took a sip from his coffee. "Take another tour after dark. Believe me, I grew up around here."

"Anyway," Tubby continued, "my friend Janie Caragliano runs the Monkey Business tavern and is getting grief for staging live music at night. Apparently there's a problem with the quality of life officer in this district."

"Right."

"Do you know that particular cop and, you know, what my approach should be?"

"As for approach, I don't know what you're talking about," Babineaux said. "But I do know the cop. You passed her when you came in. Tall? White shirt?"

"Oh, yeah. So that's what a quality of life officer looks like. What's her name?"

"Officer Smith."

"First name?"

"Jane, possibly. Nothing you'd remember."

"How would I get in touch with her?"

"Just call the station and leave a message."

Tubby thought he had gotten about as much help as a cup of coffee would buy. But as long as he was here…

"Here's another question," he persisted, though Ireanous checked his watch. "Where would I go to find records about a crime, a murder actually, that happened a long time ago?"

"How long?"

"About forty years ago."

"You're going to have trouble with that, buddy. But the place to start would be at Central Records at Tulane and Broad."

"Do you know anybody there who could help me?"

Officer Babineaux laughed. "It happens that I do. Rick Sandoval. He's also being punished for being too good of a cop. Central records is police Hell."

"Sandoval? Listen, I really appreciate this."

"Hope it helps." Ireanous must have seen something about Tubby that he liked because he suddenly became more friendly. "What kind of lawyer are you?" he asked.

"I do all sorts of things. Civil and criminal," Tubby said vaguely. "My clients always seem to have multiple problems." It was true.

"Well, here's one you'll like. What do you think about a cop who breaks a guy's jaw with just one punch? It's in the line of duty, you might say. You think that's an assault?"

"Sure, it's an assault. But you're a cop. If the punch was justified, that's what we pay you for."

"I was definitely justified. But now my ass is in a crack about it."

"Don't you have a union? I thought they would defend you against anything."

"Not in my case. It's technically an association, not a union, and here's the thing, the guy I popped is the president."

"Oh, that's bad."

"Tell me about it. I'm possibly facing criminal charges."

"Have you talked to a lawyer about this?"

Ireanous ran his palm over his smooth scalp. "I am right now."

"Hang on," Tubby said. "There's more to it than that. You

haven't asked me to represent you, and I haven't agreed to do it either."

"Flowers said you're a winner, but that you don't work for free."

Tubby nodded his head. No argument there.

"What's your fee?" the policeman asked, stroking the holstered gun on his belt for comfort.

"It varies a great deal," Tubby said. "It all depends on what I have to do."

"What would you charge for, what do you lawyers say, an initial consultation?"

Tubby made up a number.

"I can do that," Ireanous said.

Tubby wished he had gone higher. "Can you come to my office?" he asked.

"I guess so. Where is it? I have to go to work now."

Tubby gave the directions and they shook hands.

"I can give you Jane Smith's cell phone number," Ireanous said gruffly as they walked out to the street together.

Outside there was an orange parking ticket on Tubby's windshield. The cop laughed and waved goodbye.

Tubby tossed the ticket into his glove compartment and pulled out his phone. Jane Smith didn't pick up, but Tubby left his number and asked her to call. Driving slowly , he looked in the recessed doorways of Chartres Street for the mystery meter maid, but she was well hidden.

Next stop was Tulane and Broad, a destination Tubby knew well. He found a parking spot in a pay-lot full of Lincolns and BMWs, dented pick-ups and old Impalas, representing the spectrum of who came to this place. There were those here voluntarily—hustling lawyers—and those who were here against their will—sad and poor defendants. Tubby took a deep breath to ready himself for this world: city blocks packed with jail buildings, sketchy bail bondsmen, the towering criminal courthouse with its bold stone relief of what appeared to be an African-American cannoneer turning away in shame from an armed Caucasian civilian and a Louisiana statesman, the municipal and traffic courts dedicated to delivering justice to the proletariat, the Police Department, the District Attorney, and the loud city buses belching clouds of exhaust.

He ran across busy Broad Street together with a cluster of women and little children all evidently headed to the fortress-like gates of Orleans Parish Prison for visiting day. Separating from his crowd he made his way through a concrete plaza, baking hot and filled with memorials to slain officers, to police headquarters and presented himself inside at the information desk.

There he was informed that the office he was looking for was called the Records and Identification Division, first floor to your right. Through wide glass doors there was a long tin-topped counter. It was staffed by a receptionist who sat behind a computer with a cash register immediately beside her. She peered at him, her only victim, over her reading glasses.

"I'm looking for some old police records," Tubby said. "Am I in the right place?"

"Yes, sir," the receptionist said tonelessly. "You might want to review this brochure first, and then I'll be happy to explain the process further."

She plucked a blue and silver pamphlet from a stack and handed it to her customer with a tight smile. It took Tubby only a few seconds to figure out that he had to put in a "public records request," that it would take some unspecified period of time before the Custodian of Records determined which of the records he sought were public and which were protected by a Constitutional right of individual privacy, or were "police work product," and most importantly, what the appropriate fee was.

Helpfully, there was a comprehensive and not inexpensive schedule of fees for procuring copies of everything.

"I guess you don't give out much for free," he said.

"I'm sorry? What did you say?"

Tubby pocketed the brochure. "I meant to say, is Officer Rick Sandoval here?"

"Yes, he is," she said, with misgivings she wanted him to know about. "Your name, sir?"

He told her and stared absently at the walls of file cabinets while she made a call.

A few minutes passed before a brown-haired policeman with straight shoulders, the chest of a weight lifter, and a crisp blue uniform, came out of the stacks. He took his sweet time walking up to the desk.

"How can I help you?" he asked, as if he didn't think he could. He was erect and good-looking, but not young.

"I got your name from Ireanous…"

Sandoval coughed loudly. "Come on, over here." He moved further down the counter out of the receptionist's earshot. "Let's not block Missus Mogilles' desk."

They shifted fifteen feet away. Sandoval leaned in with his elbows on the dented counter-top.

"Let's try that again," he said.

Tubby also bent over, a co-conspirator. Their foreheads almost touched.

"Ireanous Babineaux. I asked him how I could locate some old police records, and he gave me your name."

"What's he to you?"

"I'm a lawyer. He might or might not end up being a client of mine. But this has nothing to do with his situation. This inquiry is personal."

"By situation, you mean him busting up that crud Alonzo's

pretty smile?" Sandoval's voice came out of lips that were barely parted and a whiskery square jaw that didn't move.

Tubby shrugged.

"How old is the case? I mean, if it's historical a lot of those records are online at the Public Library."

"Nineteen seventies."

"That ain't old. That's when I was a kid."

Tubby gave him a smile. "I'm about the same age as you, and it's still a long time ago to me. I saw a kid get shot. I tried to save him, but I couldn't. I've always wanted to know what really happened."

"What was it? Some kind of a robbery?"

"An anti-war protest."

Sandoval grunted. "I did my part in Grenada on Operation Urgent Fury."

"I was in the Army. Military Police," Tubby said.

Sandoval thought it over. "Tell you what. Give me what you've got on the incident, and I'll see what I can find. Give me a number where I can reach you."

"Thanks. I don't want to cause you any trouble."

That got a laugh.

"They already got me working in in a file room where nobody gets any files. I get to take the bus to work. I'll be passed over for promotion this year. What more can they do to me?"

* * *

After leaving Sandoval, Tubby hung out in the reception area of the police building where it was air-conditioned. He checked his phone. Nothing from Jane Smith, the quality of life officer, so he called her one more time. This time she answered. Her voice was clipped and official. He explained that he represented Janie Caragliano, the owner of the Monkey Business Club.

"You're an attorney?"

He admitted that he was.

"We don't usually talk to attorneys."

"Well, I'm really just a concerned citizen, and Janie is an old friend of mine. I'm only trying to find out what the problem is. We want to get it corrected."

"She's only gotten about five notices of violations."

"Really? She didn't give any of them to me."

"They were all properly mailed and posted."

"I'm sure they were," Tubby hastily agreed, "but something must have happened to them. Could I come to your office to pick up copies and see what this is all about?"

"Not unless you get here in the next thirty minutes. I have a community meeting to go to at two o'clock."

"Sure. Fifth District headquarters is where?"

"Thirty-nine hundred North Claiborne."

"No problem." Back to the same neighborhood where his day had begun. He checked in with Cherrylynn, told her about his upcoming meeting the next day with Officer Babineaux, and asked her to open a file and prepare a contract for the client to sign. She was pleased to learn that he was working.

"What's the nature of the representation?" she asked.

"Put down police brutality."

"Oh, good. We haven't had one of those for a while."

"Are you in class tomorrow?"

"No, not till Thursday afternoon," she said.

"Good. I'd like you to go online, or go over to the New Orleans public library if you have to and look at their microfilm. See what you can find out about a death-by-gunshot that occurred on or about…" He had to check a note in his pocket for the date.

"What's the name."

"I never actually knew his full name. He went by 'Parker.' "

She was doubtful of success but agreed to try. Tubby was sure she would succeed. He had great faith in Cherrylynn's research abilities.

The Fifth District precinct station was a lot easier to locate than the morning's coffee shop, and any doubts you were in the right place were washed away by the twenty-or-so blue and white cruisers parked outside a functional concrete orange and cream-colored building with windows too small to jump out of.

Jane Smith did in fact have an office, but it was a tiny one with a tiny desk and no windows. There was a blue plastic chair in front of the desk, and the officer waved him into it.

"Here's the copies you wanted." She pushed a few papers across the desk along with a brown envelope he could use to carry them in.

"I appreciate your speedy service," he said. "What's the gist?"

"Two gists, actually," she replied drily. "The neighbors have complained about the noise level and have even sent me some of the decibel readings they took. The other gist is that the property isn't allowed to have live music at all under the new Comprehensive Zoning Ordinance."

"Wait a second. I thought the whole question about how loud music clubs could be was still being debated. And isn't the new zoning ordinance still pending final approval?"

"Yes, but no matter which decibel level applies—and you are correct, everybody seems to have an opinion about which level is best—this bar is exceeding it."

"If you believe the neighbors' readings. Have you done your own?"

"Our equipment has been broken for a month, but I was out there last Saturday morning at six a.m. and the music drowned out the garbage trucks coming down the street."

The lawyer stroked his chin, pondering.

"And as far as the zoning plan," Smith continued, "that side of the block is zoned residential and light commercial and no one gets to sell alcohol or present live entertainment to the public unless they are grandfathered in."

"Which means, the bar has to have been in continuous operation for a long time?"

"Right, and she's only been open for a year."

"Well, it was closed for a while because of Katrina. There's an exception for that."

"You are correct again, but before the hurricane that building was a residence."

"No, ma'am, it was a bar."

"No, sir, it was a residence."

"So is that the real issue?"

"Correct. That and the loud music they play. It doesn't help that crowds of college students congregate there at all hours and urinate in the neighbors' bushes."

Tubby was about to ask what evidence she had of that, but he caught himself in time.

Janie, it seemed, had a series of regulatory hearings coming up over the next two weeks, and that was all she wrote. The complaining neighbors' names were not on the notices.

XI

Raisin was enjoying the early show at Monkey Business. A solo artist was on stage, a spectrally thin man whose bushy white beard hid his mouth, and almost his nose and eyes as well, belting out the blues and loudly strumming a twelve-string steel guitar. His amp was the size of a small microwave but still made plenty of sound as he worked through "Mannish Boy."

Raisin's date was there with him, the oil company engineer who had given him his car. She'd told Raisin she truthfully didn't care much for the music, but he figured she liked him a lot. Her name was Sadie, and exploring the cultural depths of New Orleans with this weathered but entertaining man with the soft curly black hair seemed to suit her just fine.

"The artist certainly looks like he lives his music," she whispered into her boyfriend's ear.

"That's Scotch he's sipping from that paper cup," Raisin whispered back. "And believe me, honey, we're gonna have lots of fun." He stroked her neck lightly with his fingers, then went back to drinking. He had bought them each a beer and an order of cheese fries to share, which was about the limit of the financial contribution he planned to make to the night's entertainment.

"Tell me about your day," she said hopefully.

"I did some work on the boat. Mostly just cleaning it up."

She was envious. "I bet it felt wonderful to be outdoors and on the Lake."

"Yeah, it was. What did you do today?"

"Still working on the Centurion Project. Four months to installation, and the countdown is on. Mostly, I was in meetings all day, but I did get to take a short walk on my lunch break. I went over to Lafayette Square and, you know, just looked around."

"You love what you do," he said understandingly.

"There are some days I wish I could just hang out like you, uh…" she bit her lip. "I mean hang out with you." She patted his leg, looking to see if she had hurt his feelings.

Not a chance. Raisin's hide was tough. He changed the subject.

"I saw a funny billboard today driving up by the lake," he said. "It was for Ochsner Hospital. It says, 'Ochsner, #1 in the Nation for Liver transplants.'" He chuckled.

"I don't get it."

"Kind of a New Orleans specialty, don't you think?"

"Raisin dear, you see things nobody else would see."

"It's my complicated mind that keeps you interested." He reached into his shirt pocket where his cigarettes usually were, then remembered he had quit.

"That's right," she agreed, and she meant it.

"Where's Janie tonight?" Raisin asked the barkeep, who had come over to check on them.

"She's upstairs," the young man answered. "Is your lawyer friend coming over?"

"Should be here any minute."

"She told me to let her know."

At that moment Tubby appeared beside Sadie's elbow and she offered him her cheek for a quick peck.

"How is everybody?" he asked.

"Life is good," Raisin said, raising his voice to be heard over the tinny wails of the steel guitar.

"I don't see why anybody would complain about the noise level in here," Tubby yelled. "It's just normal New Orleans music to me."

"I think they'll have other stuff going on later. The sign says 'Last Rites at 11.' " He pointed to a pair of big Bose amplifiers, unplugged but waiting, at the rear of the stage. "This blues man is just the early show."

Janie showed up behind the bar, a ring of silk flowers around the brim of her Stetson. Her bosom strained against the buttons of her khaki shirt. "What are y'all drinking?" she bellowed.

"I'll have an Old Fashioned," Tubby called over the counter, "if he can make one."

"I don't know about Jack, but I can. You kids want another beer?"

Raisin and Sadie both nodded.

The blues singer launched into "Seventh Son."

"Have you ever measured the decibels in here," Tubby asked Janie when she set the tawny red concoction in front of him on its tiny napkin.

"They keep talking about decibels, decibels," she complained. "What are they anyway, and how do know how many you got?"

"It's a measure of sound level. I guess you use some kind of meter," Tubby opined.

"Where would you get one? Is there a sound store?"

"I don't know," he admitted.

"I could ask around at work," Sadie offered.

"What about your friend Jason Boaz?" Raisin suggested. "Isn't he some kind of engineer? He's a tinkerer and probably knows all about any crazy device you can think of. Or he could probably just invent one."

That wasn't a bad idea. Jason was an occasional client of Tubby's. He invented things, like radios that masked the origin of email messages, apps that could tell you where your boss was standing in the office, blenders that could turn peach pits into livestock feed. Some were less likely to make it than others but those that did earned good money.

The blues singer got to the end of his set, to scattered applause. He came around the room with a tip jar. "Great sound," said Tubby and tossed in a five. Sadie threw in a bill, and Raisin passed. Someone plugged in the jukebox and out came George Jones. But, comparatively speaking, the joint was quiet, and private conversations were able to resume.

Tubby stood up and stretched. "I guess I'll call Jason while I'm thinking about it. Let's see what he knows about measuring decibels."

* * *

The man with the troubled past was styling his hair with an ergonomic clipper he had invented. It fit into the palm of his hand and was elongated to reach behind the head. He had a date tonight with Norella Peruna, a Honduran who often looked him up when she was in New Orleans without her current husband, whoever he might be. She had briefly been a widow when Max Finn died, but after that misfortune, she had soon walked down the aisle again. Norella liked a good time, as in casinos, fancy Latin dance parties, the tango, shopping at the outlet malls, and Jason tried his best to oblige her. Tonight he had a pair of tickets to the Azúcar Ball in the lobby of the Whitney Bank, a charity event with a big band that went on till dawn.

Of course, he was almost certain to run into some of the old crowd, but they normally ignored him. Because he wrote generous checks, when he was flush with cash, to the correct liberation organizations and churches, he was afforded some peace and quiet.

He heard the phone buzzing in the kitchen but declined to answer it. It took major concentration to trim his chin and cheeks and leave just the right aura of heavy whiskers, and only the slightest suggestion of a beard.

* * *

Tubby left a message and dropped the phone back in his pocket.

"Oh well, Janie, we'll do something about all these decibels in good time. But to a more important problem, what was in this building before Katrina? The city is saying it was a residence."

"No way!" she exclaimed. "Bud lived upstairs with his second wife and his mother, just like I do now, but this down here was always a club."

"Yes!" Tubby slapped the bar. "That's what we need to prove. Have you got any pictures?"

"Are you kidding me? This whole joint was under water. There was black mold from the floor to the roof. Hell, the roof blew off! But Bud always told me this downstairs was a happening bar. They always played live music here. Hell, his mother was a belly dancer!"

"Okay, tell me some names. Who played here?"

"I don't know. He didn't tell me. But they had some big shows. He talked about a New Year's party that got raided."

"That's probably not too helpful. How about the neighborhood? Anybody here likely to remember?"

"The neighbors here are all new. Back in Bud's day, this whole area was white. Then the yats moved to Kenner, darlin'.

This was one of the last white bars. Not too many people were coming. At the end Bud was running it as a private club."

"To keep it all white?"

"Shit, no! Bud wasn't even all white. He was one of those blended Mediterranean types. He didn't give a crap what color you were. He didn't like wops, that's about it. But to get the customers in here he had to offer extra entertainment."

"You mean like…"

"I mean like girls."

"This was a strip club?" Tubby exclaimed.

"It might have been that." Janie lowered her voice. "But to be real about it, baby, this old joint was a back-of-town whore-house!"

Raisin's laugh was like a dog's bark. "Let's see you get a zoning variance for that," he crowed. He happily tipped back his beer.

"A what-house?" Sadie was delighted.

"Jeez," Tubby said. "That could give us a problem."

"But," Janie insisted, voice rising, "they had live music here on the weekends. I swear!"

XII

Cherrylynn had oatmeal with walnuts and cranberries at McDonald's on St. Charles Avenue while studying a philosophy lecture on her iPad. This breakfast was a huge splurge. She usually ate low-fat yogurt, berries, and bran with almond milk at her apartment, and would normally be at her desk by now. But this morning she was traveling on business and was entitled to get to the office late. The public library didn't open until ten. And she would get reimbursed for the meal.

She wasn't getting all this "Utilitarianism." Virtue lies in a thing achieving its purpose? So, the oats achieved their purpose by being oatmeal? This was just her third week of class and her professor had promised that they would be moving fast into the post-moderns and the existentialists and the phenomenologists, "where nothing means anything at all," he said. She certainly hoped so, because she was already getting stuck.

Cherrylynn tossed her red hair back and wrapped it up behind her neck with a rubber tie while reading the last page of the lecture. This oatmeal hit the spot, though some of the customers in here were a little sketchy. One kid with an extra-large black T-shirt stuffed into his baggy black pants shuffled in to order a vanilla ice cream cone for breakfast. He got it and shuffled back out without being asked to pay. A couple of cops were arguing loudly over their Big Breakfasts about the score of a high school football game. As their voices rose, she was a little alarmed that they were both armed.

According to her watch, it was time to go. She grabbed her gear and ran out to wait for the streetcar. Almost immediately the green car came rambling down the tracks. She hopped on to find a typical morning crowd of people headed downtown to work. One nice guy offered her a seat. He had combed blond hair and was wearing a gray suit and tie and eyeglasses with heavy black frames. She accepted with almost a curtsy and a blush. They locked eyes for a poignant minute as the streetcar lurched forward and zipped along. By the time she jumped off the car in the CBD at Gravier Street she had already learned that the guy's name was Carl, that he had just passed the bar, and that he was working at the Corrigan and Dutch law firm. He did admiralty. She divulged her own place of employment. Maybe they would see each other around. She considered coming late to work more often.

The main library had automatic doors that only worked sometimes. Inside was a sleepy guard to keep you from stealing books and an array of lost and homeless patrons wanting to stay out of the weather. But on the third floor there was the Louisiana Collection, with thousands of books and papers too rare to ever be checked out. Cherrylynn had spent hours and hours here before, doing projects for her boss, and she liked the quiet and seriousness of the room and the many intriguing items the collection contained. This was the real stuff worth preserving. The library was moving toward digital, and must have gotten a large grant to buy the rows of new computers set out for the patrons to use, but it also had several tall black microfilm readers. You could pick out a four-inch reel of tape, fix it upon the spindles, then slowly wind it under a bright light. It was like watching an old black and white movie—page after page, for instance, of old New Orleans newspapers.

The films were in gray file drawers against the wall, organized by date, and it took Cherrylynn only a few minutes to find the reel she wanted. Several machines were available. She picked one that looked like it would work, clicked on the light, and loaded up her reel. The past flashed before her.

General Creighton Abrams is to replace General William Westmorland. He asks for more troops. The Orioles, Red Sox and Tigers are all competing for the American League East. In local news, the first Southern Decadence Party is held at Matassa's Bar in the French Quarter. Hurricane Agnes is expected to cause damage in Pennsylvania. D.H. Holmes has a summer sale on ivory silk organza and lace wedding gowns at $229.99. The New Dick Van Dyke Show comes on at seven p.m. on CBS. Manuel's Hot Tamale carts are available, vendors keep half of what they sell.

The hard part of this research was getting distracted by all the vintage cars, the fantastically cheap prices, and the under-dressed models in the department store ads. They wore bell bottoms or miniskirts. Cherrylynn stared at the drawings of their pencil-thin legs with fascination. And look at that ad for the red Corvette! Was that phallic or what? "Phallic" was a word her art history teacher threw into almost every other paragraph of her lectures.

She found the right day of the month. The headline was, "Secretary of State Speaks at the World Trade Center." There were other big stories that day, but nothing in the front section about an anti-war demonstration or a shooting. She tried Metro. Nothing there, either. Maybe the evening paper. Nope, nothing there.

To be thorough, she scrolled ahead to the next day. "Governor Edwards Appoints Wife to U.S. Senate." Not rele-vant. Nothing in the front section. Then, in Metro, under "Police Reports," she saw, "An unidentified shooting victim was brought to Charity Hospital. Anyone with any information contact Detective P. Kronke at 555-2174."

"Bingo!" She snapped her finger. "I am one sharp cookie!"

She took a picture of the screen when she was sure the librarian wasn't looking.

* * *

Officer Ireanous Babineaux showed up at Dubonnet & Associates as scheduled, in uniform and carrying his hat under his arm. Cherrylynn showed him in, trying to put him at ease, but he sat down in Tubby's big visitor's armchair as upright as a porch column.

"Any trouble parking?" Tubby asked, to warm things up.

"Nope. Parked in front of your building on St. Charles Avenue with my flashers on."

"You evidently don't have to worry about getting tickets."

"Never," Ireanous said flatly.

"Very good. Tell me what's going on."

"How confidential is this?"

"Technically speaking, not very, at least not yet. But I take a bit of a different view. Nothing you tell me leaves this room, unless you're about to commit a crime."

The policeman gave a hearty laugh. Tubby smiled back.

"Okay, this guy, Archie Alonzo, the head of our policeman's association, has never liked me. I beat his ass once in high school over a girl, his sister in fact, and he has never gotten over it. So they reorganized our department last spring, you may have read about it, and suddenly nobody can work a private detail without going through a so-called central system. Which actually doesn't work, and they don't care who your existing clients are, but they might be people you've worked with for years."

"A private detail? You mean like guarding a bar?"

"They don't let you work bars anymore—not in uniform. That's supposed to put cops in close proximity to bad guys, which is a no-no. So now, we have to guess who the bad guys are. But we work everything else. Parties, weddings, funerals, festivals. The easiest job is being a crossing guard for a private school. Working details is the only way you can make any money in our line of work. Do you know what the pay scale is for cops?"

"Not much, I bet."

"You got that right. They changed the rules for who can take what private job, but there's been a lot of confusion lately. So I kept on doing the same private jobs I've always done, and some dweeb turned me in. I filed a grievance and Alonzo, our union president, told me to my face that I'm fucked. He says he won't lift a finger. And in his day he stole thousands of dollars on private details. One thing led to another and I smacked him."

"You broke his jaw?"

Ireanous laughed, even deeper this time. "One punch and down he went. The guy always has been soft."

"Who swung first?"

There was a pause.

"Well, he made a threatening gesture."

"Like what?"

"He jabbed me in the chest with his finger."

"That's good. What's your current status in the department?"

"I'm just biding my time, waiting for my hearing, living the good life in the Ninth Ward."

"Where were you before?"

"Uptown at Magazine and Napoleon."

"That was better?"

"Much."

"Less crime?"

"Sure, and lots better criminals."

"When's your hearing?"

"Who the hell knows. Whenever Internal Affairs feels like burning me."

"All this just for working an unauthorized private detail? What was it?"

"I was, uh, bodyguard for Trey Caponata?"

Tubby knew that name. "The old man's son?"

"Yeah."

"The mob boss's son?"

"That was just a rumor," Babineaux said. "The mob is history anyway."

Tubby shook his head. "Nuts. I met the old guy just one time and there was no question that I was breathing only because it pleased him to see me sweat."

Ireanous shrugged.

"So that's it?" Tubby asked.

"No," the cop said. "Not quite. I also run, I should say ran, the organization that assigned the private details to the other cops."

"You mean you were in charge of who got the jobs?"

"Pretty much. Other people kept track of the schedules and the books."

"Running such an organization must have taken up a lot of your time."

The potential client nodded.

"Did you have any left over for police work?"

The scowl, the growl and the slap on the desk erupted all at the same time.

"I was and am a damn good cop!" Babineaux thundered.

There was a light tap, tap, tapping on the door.

74

"Come in," Tubby said softly.

Cherrylynn's face appeared, radiating concern. "Anyone need any coffee?" she asked.

"No, we're fine," Tubby said. She backed out and closed the door quickly.

"Are you married?" he asked the policeman.

"Divorced."

"Any kids?"

"I've got a daughter. She's in college, but when she's home she lives with me."

"Where is she in school?"

"Florida State. She wants to be a doctor."

Tubby sighed. "Okay. I will represent you. Here's a contract to look over." On the document was a blank space where Tubby could write in his hourly fee. He filled that in with a high number and slid the paper over the desk. "Take it home and read it if you like."

"I can read it here."

And he did. It was just two pages long, but it took about ten minutes, while Tubby stared out the window at the French Quarter far below. A long string of barges filled with Kentucky coal was being guided downstream around the hairpin turn in the Mississippi River by a red tugboat. Ultimate destination, Spain.

"You get a retainer?" the cop asked.

"I do."

"What the hell," his new client said. "I'll sign."

"Excellent," Tubby said. He took back the executed contract and signed it himself. "You can take care of the retainer with Cherrylynn. Now, what kind of paperwork do you have about your assault. I mean, altercation? A write-up? A copy of your grievance? Anything official?"

Ireanous had an envelope in his pocket and handed it over.

"Did I hear you say that Rick Sandoval over in the Police Records office was somehow connected to this?"

"He was in charge of collecting money for the details from the customers and paying it over to the cops."

"I guess you guys took a cut."

"Absolutely. We ran a legitimate business."

* * *

As soon as his new client left, Tubby called Flowers.

"Tell me anything you can about Trey Caponata."

"Hello to you." Flowers' voice was smooth, almost a like song, with a hint of a Spanish accent. "Caponata is a small time gangster as far as I know. A Mafia-wannabe. His father ran the mob through reputation and fear, but I don't think the son has ever filled those shoes. I expect he pimps some girls and fences stolen goods, but nothing big-time. Why?"

"My new client, Ireanous Babineaux, was his bodyguard."

Flowers whistled. "That I didn't know. Babineaux has not actually been a close friend of mine or anything. He has, however, been a source of valuable information for me over the years."

"You paid him?"

"That's an unusual question coming from you, Tubby, but, yes, in a manner of speaking."

"I'm sorry. I didn't mean to pry into your business. Why would Caponata need a bodyguard?"

"My guess is just for show. Want me to check him out more thoroughly?"

"Yes, I do. And also see what background you can get for me on the head of the police union. Archie, maybe Archibald, I don't know, Alonzo."

"Right. I can tell you right away that Alonzo is politically connected. He may have dirtier hands than the young Capo-nata. But I'll pull together some details for you."

"Good. As soon as possible, please."

"You got it. I'm glad to get back on a case with you."

Tubby was glad, too. The only problem was that Flowers was expensive. He had better bill this client regularly.

* * *

"Mister Boaz is on the line," Cherrylynn told him. Tubby picked up.

"Good morning, Jason."

"It's noon. I just won three thousand dollars at the off-track. I'm about to walk into Galatoire's 33 and buy a steak. You want to be my guest?"

Tubby certainly did.

"Out to lunch," he shouted to Cherrylynn as he bolted out the door.

* * *

She had been waiting to tell him about her trip to the library. It was so frustrating to be in the middle of some real detective work and have to sit on your hands. Mister Dubonnet might not be back for hours. She was tapping her foot impatiently when the phone rang.

"Is Dubonnet there?"

"I'm sorry, sir, but he's out. Who's calling?"

"This is Officer Sandoval at Police Records. When will he be back?"

"I'm afraid he's in court and may be gone for hours."

"I've got something for him."

"If you tell me what it is, I'll be sure to let him know when he gets back."

"It's a package, and I don't like keeping it around here."

"I am Mister Dubonnet's confidential secretary. If it is important I can pick up the package myself and see that it's kept in a safe place."

"I'd say it's important to him. I'm at police headquarters."

"I could be there in about twenty minutes."

"I'll be outside on the steps taking a cigarette break."

Cherrylynn wasted no time locking up and grabbing an elevator. There was a cab stand down at the street.

XIII

Tubby swung open the gold-handled door at the restaurant on Bourbon Street and was immediately soothed by the elegant décor, the magnificently long bar, and the subdued lights and soft ragtime music. This was an offshoot of the original Galatoire's next door, which the lawyer regarded as one of the finest establishments on the planet, but not the sort of place you went to on a whim. He saw Jason sitting with his back to the mahogany-paneled wall. He had an ample martini to his lips. He stood up to greet Tubby, showing how tall and thin he was. Though his beard and black hair were neat, the heavy black-framed glasses he wore and his rumpled trousers and jacket made him look like a college professor.

"Gin or vodka?" Tubby asked. He slid into a chair to face his host.

"A Beefeater's, my friend. What's your poison?"

"I'll follow suit." A waiter appeared. "Whatever the gentleman is having," Tubby instructed. He laid the proffered menu aside. "You had a good day with the ponies?"

"A very good day. A little filly named Trailer Trash came in to win the third race at Saratoga at thirteen to one. I've been following her for weeks, and she's always coming in fourth or fifth, every single race. I figured the jockeys were holding her back, and I was right. I nailed that one, then, bless my heart, I won the daily double!"

"Very exciting." Tubby also liked nothing better than a day at the races, but he wasn't a fan of off-track betting parlors. They were now basically given over to video poker and slot machines. The traditional clientele had disappeared almost entirely. "How often do you wager?" he asked.

"I dabble in something every day. It's an addiction, I know. I keep two bookies busy. I even gambled online for a while, but then I got hacked. That was a learning experience."

The waiter came back with a pair of drinks and offered to take their orders.

"A sixteen-ounce strip, garçon." Jason tossed back his first drink and reached for his fresh one. "Medium rare. And your *potatoes au gratin* and brown butter mushrooms."

Tubby scanned the menu quickly.

"I'll try your House Boudin-Stuffed Roasted Quail."

"With a salad or soup?"

"Why yes, please. I'll have your turtle soup."

"What about the horseradish-crusted bone marrow?" Jason asked.

"Sounds fulfilling, doesn't it, but not today. I'd better stick to my diet."

"Save some space for the peach cobbler. It's pretty damn good."

"Let's do this every week," his guest suggested.

Jason laughed and took another gulp. "Now, what did you call me about?"

"An old friend of mine owns a bar and music club."

"No surprise there."

"Yeah. Well, she needs to be able to measure the decibel levels outside her bar while a band is playing. I thought you might have an idea about how to do that."

"You use a sound level meter, which I imagine you can probably buy at Radio Shack. Above ninety decibels, something like that, is bad for you." Jason turned thoughtful. "But that seems like a very old-school way to go about it. How can you demonstrate what and where you took a reading?"

He pulled out his phone and began thumbing away.

"You know, I don't see that there's an app being offered for this." He started humming.

"What are you talking about?"

"It seems to me that what you'd want, for evidentiary purposes as it were, is an app that lets you take a picture of the bar in real time and display the decibel rating on the screen in a way you could save it. It would record the place, the time and the sound. But I don't see that such an app is available."

"Too bad."

"Not bad at all. I'll play around with this tonight and see if I can't create one. Who knows, this could be another big idea."

"Don't forget where you got it."

Jason resurfaced to focus on Tubby. He laughed. "You don't even know what an app is," he said.

"Of course I do." Jason spared him from having to display the limits of his knowledge by launching into a discourse on his date with Norella. They had danced till three in the morning and made love on her living room floor. At least that's what Jason thought had happened.

Before more was revealed, the food arrived.

"Hot plates," the waiter warned. Jason's steak sizzled. Tubby's quail steamed. They stopped talking for a few minutes and ate. The small toasty brown bird was served on a glacé of black cherries and wilted spinach, and with the rice sausage spilling onto the plate it sent out mists of wonderful spicy flavors. It was a shame to pierce it with a fork.

"Mine's excellent. How's your steak?" Tubby finally managed to ask.

"*Très Bien.* So, what else are you working on these days? Any more New Orleans political intrigues or gruesome murders?"

"One of each, actually. The intrigue may involve organized crime and our city police department. I shouldn't have taken the case, but it promises to be another fascinating glimpse into what makes our very warm and moist small town work. The murder, on the other hand, happened forty years ago, and is personal to me."

"Really? Who got killed?"

"A young boy. I never actually learned his full name. They called him Parker. It was at a public demonstration. I was there. Someone pulled up in a car and shot him."

Jason's ruddy face paled. He took a pull on his drink and signaled the waiter for a refill.

"This was back in the days of anti-war demonstrations. I just happened to get involved during a brief but very, uh, experimental period in my life."

"You were there when it happened?" Jason's voice sounded strained.

"Yeah. The kid died, practically in my arms. I never knew who did it or why. Is there something wrong with your food?"

Jason had quietly set down his fork, and he dropped his chin as if in prayer.

"How do you plan to find the answers to your questions?"

"I'll dig up what can be dug up. Granted, it was a long time ago. But I'm a resourceful person."

Jason raised his head and met Tubby's eyes.

"You should leave this in the past, my friend. The people who did this are loco crazy. They were crazy then, and they are crazy now."

Tubby was astonished. "You actually know something about this event?"

Jason just shook his head sadly.

* * *

The taxi dropped Cherrylynn off on Broad across the street from the jail. She had to fork over most of her cash because the swarthy driver with the tiny mustache claimed that his credit card machine was broken. Flustered, she hurried up the wide steps and spied, across the plaza, a sentry-like uniformed police-man who was indeed smoking a cigarette. Getting closer, she observed that he was surrounded by a ring of smashed butts which blended into the gum-stained concrete. He was holding a manila envelope.

"Officer Sandoval?" she inquired.

He looked her up and down and grunted, "You ain't bad looking."

"I'm Mister Dubonnet's secretary," she said, inexplicably not feeling insulted by his forwardness. "Do you have some-thing for him?"

The policeman stuck out his arm, big as both of hers, and handed over the envelope.

"Tell him this is all there is." He shrugged. "It was a long time ago and things get lost. This is the original file, and I'd like it back."

Sandoval ground what was left of his smoke into the pavement with all the rest.

"Nice to meet you, Miss Secretary." He turned abruptly and walked back into the glass building.

"Thank you," Cherrylynn called after him.

She turned the envelope over. There were no markings on it. She noted that the flap was clipped shut but not sealed.

Holding it against her chest with an elbow, she searched through her purse until she found a dollar and a quarter. Great! At least she could afford to take a bus back downtown.

Soon, sitting in air-conditioned comfort on the crowded Number 30, she gave in to temptation and unfastened the clasp. She peeked inside. There was a ragged worn folder—so this was indeed the original—and just a few pieces of paper. The top one had a Police Department letterhead.

Her seatmate, a fat lady with a Bible on her lap, was watching this out of the corner of her eye. Cherrylynn closed the envelope and stared out the window at the chicken shacks and drug clinics they were rolling past. She hopped off on St. Charles Avenue and was unlocking the DUBONNET & ASSOCIATES offices five minutes later. Obviously, Tubby had not yet returned.

No doubt the boss would expect her to inventory the contents and transfer them into a file. This would also satisfy her curiosity. She extracted the pages and spread them out on her desk.

Here's what she found:

A worn dirty manila file folder with a tag pasted to it that read: "No. JDX2374."

A form releasing the body of John Doe to the Dennis Mortuary on Louisiana Avenue, signed by Frank Minyard, the Parish Coroner.

A copy of a piece of paper with a handwritten name on it. It was Bert Haggarty, followed by "Indiana."

The official Police Department document was a short report. It had one paragraph, denoted as "SUMMARY." It read:

"Deceased John Doe, wounds possibly self-inflicted. Subversive anti-war buttons, vagrant, possible altercation with unknown parties. Possible drug deal. One marijuana cigarette in pants pocket, sent to evidence. Prints taken. No known match. Photo of body shows gunshot."

There was no marijuana cigarette, and there were no prints. There was no photograph of the body.

Cherrylynn inspected the pages carefully. She turned them over and scanned the backs. Nothing. The manila folder, except for the file number and a small blue ink doodle on the inside that resembled a spider, was blank. But wait, near the doodle there was an indentation likely made by a pen or pencil writing on something with the folder underneath. She got out the magnifying glass she sometimes used to check her skin and made out a name. It appeared to be "Carlos Pancera," and beside that a phone number with a five-o-four area code. She jotted it down.

Cherrylynn put everything back into the envelope and locked it in her desk. After checking her phone and picking some dead leaves off the ficus plant in the corner, she couldn't think of anything else to do. So she opened up her Philosophy reading, *Critique of Pure Reason* by Immanuel Kant, and gave it a try. "That all our knowledge begins with experience there can be no doubt." Okay, so far. "So how is it possible that the faculty of cognition should be awakened into exercise other than by means of objects which affect our senses, and partly of themselves produce representation…" She closed the text. Critique of Poor Reason, maybe. She could get this, she knew. But not now.

Tapping on her laptop, she Googled "New Orleans Police Officer P. Kronke."

It didn't take long. He was in the White Pages.

* * *

At Galatoire's 33, the diners' conversation languished. What remained of their meal passed in strained silence. Jason Boaz and his guest both said no to the waiter's offer to serve them additional drinks. The last bite of quail remained on the plate. Dessert, sadly, was forgotten.

"Jason. That was a very important event in my life," Tubby pointed out, signaling the waiter that they were done. "I'm not going to let it go."

"I beg you, my friend. Let it alone."

"No. It's not going to end here," the lawyer insisted.

"*Eres hombre muerto.*"

Tubby didn't know what that meant, but he stood up.

Jason pulled out his credit card and paid while his friend left.

When the mystified boss got back to the office Cherrylynn announced, "I have some news for you."

She told him what she had learned at the library, showed him the picture she had taken of the brief death announcement in the *Times-Picayune*, and produced the file that Officer Sandoval had given her.

"He expects it back," she said, laying out the pages on the desk for him to read.

She showed him the faint scratches on the file folder and wrote out her interpretation for him.

"This is really great work," he told her. Tubby felt odd, seeing the police report and Kronke's name. It was if the past was rising back up with disturbing power, made more eerie by Jason Boaz's strange reaction at lunch. Kronke and he had crossed paths before.

"We tend to minimize the passion and danger and violence of our youth, as we get older, as we get good at adult games," he said to Cherrylynn.

They stared at each other. Neither was sure what he was talking about.

"I'm getting out of here," he said. "And I'll take this with me."

XIV

Raisin Partlow had tried to live an uncomplicated life. He had gone back to school after the war and collected his degrees, but he had never done a thing with them. His major achievements were in the realms of tennis and boating, two careers where you could wear shorts, and over the years he had formed attachments with a number of accomplished women. He was usually serious enough about a girlfriend to move in with her, which saved him a lot of overhead.

The war now came back only as fitful dreams for Raisin. It didn't actually seem true-to-life anymore, but was as if it had happened to someone else who might have died years ago. It did, however, always feature helicopters. Sometimes he was in the middle of the drama, giving the high sign on a cloudy day to a young pilot carrying a fresh rifle squad into battle. Sometimes he saw himself running out onto the tarmac when a bird flapped home carrying its cargo of bloody warriors. Sometimes a careless soldier dropped a match, and flames raced faster than they could run, and they were blown away by exploding aircraft. Those were his standard three dreams. Sometimes, he could mentally skip to the end and wake himself up.

Or, if it was bad, he yelled, or struggled, and Sadie shook him till he sat up awake.

"What was that?" she would ask him, frightened.

It didn't happen every night. Not nearly every night. Raisin totally rejected the role of victim. He had a superior life and an enviable backhand on the tennis courts. He thought about Marlboros, which he was trying to beat for the twentieth time, a lot more than he thought about Vietnam. America had had a lot of wars since then. It made him feel old to think about his own, so he made an effort not to.

He buried his face in Sadie's breasts while he caught his breath. This was just an afternoon's nap that had gotten out of control, but now he was in the embrace of a beautiful scented woman, and in the present moment he could thrive.

An hour later, when they began to think about their evening plans, Raisin remembered that he had promised Janie he would go, again, to the Monkey Business for some event that very night. But lying in the bed with Sadie, he didn't feel up to it.

Pulling a white towel around himself, he found his phone and called Tubby.

"I made a promise I can't keep," he said, and told Tubby about the benefit. It was an early show. A bunch of "fabulous musicians" were playing for free to raise money for some artist who was in jail for public indecency. Whatever that was. Something about street art. The event would show off the bar at its best. Could Tubby possibly attend? There might even be newspaper and blogger attention that would help his tavern-owning client in the important realm of community affection. Raisin was a good salesman, and Tubby said he would be sure to drop in for a few minutes.

* * *

Tubby arrived while Andy J. Forest was playing harmonica, backed up by a bass guitar and a drummer. This was good, relia-ble, high-class New Orleans music, and he relaxed immediately about the whole noise-level thing. He needed a few soothing moments after his disturbing lunch with Jason Boaz. Bad enough to spoil a stuffed quail. Bad, too, to think that Jason was linked to an old atrocity. But what stung most was being shut out by a client whom he had long thought of as a friend. This bugged him greatly. He was quick to search out a drink.

There was a big crowd in the bar. Evidently whoever was in jail had some supporters. There were actually banker types wearing suits and ties in here. Make that bowties. The artist must have tapped into a well-to-do following. The cover at the door was twenty dollars.

Tubby threaded his way to the bar and wedged himself between a tall boy with the beard of a goat-farming Mennonite and a blond woman in a tight white dress with some sparkle to it, cut above the knees, whose back was to him.

"Old Fashioned!" he yelled at Jack, who gave him a slight nod.

The Regal Beer sign flashed on and off. Andy Forest was into "God Will Understand." Tubby turned his attention to the blond woman, whose rear end was bumping against his right thigh.

She was engaged in conversation with another lady, brown-haired with a brown business suit, who looked as though she might have spent her day firing people. Her eyes happened to pass his. "Hi, ladies," he said.

The woman in the suit smiled at him. The blond looked over her shoulder and turned partway around. She was a very appealing, very attractive woman about his own age with un-usually clear skin, blue eyes, and bright red lipstick.

"Who are you?" she asked.

"My name is Tubby." He sucked in his gut and grabbed the glass that had miraculously appeared. "I'm a lawyer. You?"

"Peggy. Peggy O'Flarity." She touched her hair. "And this is Caroline."

Tubby reached over and shook Caroline's hand. Then he offered his to Peggy. "What brings you here?" he asked.

Her fingers were long and cool. He was sorry to let them go.

"I volunteer at the Contemporary Arts Center," she said a little loudly because the band was heating up. "We are one of the sponsors of this event."

"Great. I've gotta admit I'm not familiar with… the artist that this is for. What's his name?"

"Dinky Bacon. He does studio art, but he's also a street performer."

"What did he do to get into trouble?"

"He's been incorporating male burlesque into his music and sometimes in his gallery exhibitions. Basically he just got a little too naked in Jackson Square."

That was funny, and Tubby laughed. He clinked glasses with Peggy, who was drinking a beer.

"It's a great city," he said. "You come here much?"

"First time." Her mate, Caroline, had rotated to pay attention to a nearby woman with spiked purple hair and an aqua tutu. "Seems like a nice enough place," Peggy observed. "It somehow feels familiar to me."

"I think it's a great establishment," Tubby said. "I represent the owner."

"That's right, you said you were a lawyer. I don't like lawyers."

"Neither do I. Why don't you?"

"My ex, I guess." She smiled again and finished her beer.

"Let me buy a round," Tubby suggested. "I'd like to know more about our honoree and why the arts center thinks he is worth supporting."

"He's actually internationally famous," she said. "But admittedly, that's mostly through the Internet since until recently he didn't believe in displaying his pieces for sale."

"Will he be here tonight?"

"Not unless he gets out of jail. The point of this whole thing is bail money."

"I suppose he has a lawyer." A frolicking drunk smashed into them and apologized. Tubby mopped Old Fashioned off his shirt.

Peggy used her napkin to help him a little. "I suppose he must," she mused.

Tubby let the subject drop. He had enough hopeless causes. Still, it looked like a lot of twenty-dollar bills had walked through the door.

He was able to get a few more details about the lady. Peggy lived far, far away on the Northshore. Actually, she owned horses.

"I know all about horses," he boasted. He was thinking about horse races, of course. But when he was ten he had had a pony.

Her kids were scattered, one in Nashville, and one in D.C.

Her ex still lived in New Orleans in their old house. She got the horse farm. And the horses.

And Tubby got her phone number, written on the back of a CAC flyer promoting "Bourbon and Burlesque."

Peggy O'Flarity had to leave early because of her long drive home. He walked her to her car, a BMW.

Back in the bar he knew only Caroline, who was at this point fully occupied by colorful people whom Tubby didn't find to be his type. Janie never made an appearance. Tubby drifted outside to compose himself in the dark. Only a few low-decibel sounds escaped from the bar, and he could hear train cars clanking in the distance. He decided that this would be a good time to drive home, after pausing for a few slow and deep inhales of rich Mississippi River air.

When he reached his house, he found a message on his land line from Marguerite. All was still well in sunny Florida, but why hadn't she heard from him? She couldn't understand. Was he all right? She was just worried about him, that's all.

He liked his Florida lady. That much was true. The chemistry was there, but ever since she had moved south from Chicago, she seemed to have developed a nesting instinct. Naples was her nest and Tubby wasn't at all sure he wanted to be an egg.

That picture was wrong on several levels, including the one that was his life, here in New Orleans, close to his girls, his law practice, and etcetera. She was also a Yankee, but what did that matter?

Nevertheless, he didn't call her back and went to bed.

It bothered him when he woke up before six, and it bothered him while he stoked up a pot of Community coffee. Eventually, after he had made some toast and eaten a Satsuma, he hit reply and let the phone ring. To his great relief, he got her voicemail.

But he didn't leave a message.

He felt bad about that, too.

XV

The lawyer got to the office a little early, even before Cherry-lynn. After leafing through *The Advocate*, where he learned that murders in New Orleans were on a pace to match 2004, a record year for homicides, and after checking his emails, he decided to follow up on the information Cherrylynn had given him.

Tubby knew the policeman, Kronke, who back in the distant past had done the so-called investigation into the death of John Doe. In recent years this same officer had interrogated Tubby when a client showed up dead in a Place Palais elevator minutes after visiting Tubby's office on the 43rd floor. Later on still, Tubby had questioned the policeman, during the crazy period when he was on the trail of the Crime Czar. Tubby regretted that he had once told Kronke to screw himself. Maybe the policeman had forgotten that, but Tubby doubted it.

He pressed in the number that Cherrylynn had given him.

"Hello," Kronke answered. He sounded grumpy, like he had just woken up.

"Hello, detective, this is Tubby Dubonnet…"

"The attorney," Kronke said flatly.

"Hey, you remembered. It's been quite some time."

"I'm off the force, so why could you be calling me?"

"You quit?"

95

"I retired. I was out of there at sixty. All I do now is kill skeet and chase the ladies."

"Good for you. Yeah, well, I've got a couple of years to go. You know, I've still got one kid in college. So I'm still practicing law."

"Enough of this old time's sake," Kronke cut him off. "Why did you call?"

"I've gotten interested in a case, a very old one. Back in the early 1970's. There was a shooting at a demonstration on Canal Street. A young kid was killed in a drive-by."

"Really."

"I know that's a long time ago, but do you remember anything about it?"

"Why should I?"

"Because you were apparently the investigating officer."

"Who says?"

"Well, your name was in the paper. And there's a police report that says the deceased was a vagrant, maybe a dope dealer. He was pronounced dead at Charity."

"Early seventies. Sorry. I wasn't on the force until 1979. Must have been my old man."

"P. Kronke?"

"Same name. He was Peter. I'm Paul."

"Don't you think it's strange that there's no follow-up information in the record?"

"Maybe the record was lost. Or maybe that's all there was. Back in the seventies, even after I became a cop, there was a homicide every day. Every Friday and Saturday night was like a shooting gallery on the carnival midway. Even Sundays, except when the Saints came on TV. One dead, two, three. They just kept coming in."

"I remember. But there's this piece of paper in the folder

and it has a name, 'Bert Haggarty' and the word 'Indiana'. Could you make a guess what that means?"

"No."

"I thought maybe it was the boy's name, or his family's name."

"I can't help you."

"That's too bad. There's another name here. It's hard to make out. But it's Carlos Pancera. Do you know who that is?"

The line went dead.

Tubby looked at his phone. "I must have struck a nerve," he muttered. He called Jason Boaz, who also answered.

"Who is Carlos Pancera?" he asked.

"Tubby, leave this alone. You'll get us all killed."

"Well, who is he?"

"I want nothing more to do with you. I have spent my entire life getting away from these people. You are too valuable to throw yourself away on these sort of Don Quixote questions."

"You make it all seem quite dramatic."

"This is not some crime novel you are writing. This is not historical research. This is real. Think about your family."

That caught Tubby in the gut.

"I have been working on the decibel app," Boaz shifted gears, "and maybe one day I will again seek your legal advice. If you are alive to give it. In the meantime, go to Radio Shack."

Flowers phoned in. He wanted to make his report in person, and Tubby invited him to come on downtown.

While he was on the phone Cherrylynn made a pot of coffee. He filled her in on his conversation with Kronke.

"And by the way, when Flowers gets here please show him right in."

Her hands flew to her hair. He enjoyed watching her blush.

For some reason, the detective's visits always energized his secretary.

"Oh, before I forget," she said as she was closing his door. "Your friend Marguerite called and left a message."

"What was it?"

"She says she's taking a cruise to Cancun and not to be concerned about her. She said she'd let you know when she returns."

The door closed. All of a sudden Tubby was full of concerns and regrets. How could he lose Marguerite? She was such a rare and rich individual.

His remorse was short-lived. There were other important things to think about, right? Who the hell was Carlos Pancera?

And his computer told him that pleadings had been filed in Jahnke v. Grimaldi, his oilfield accident case that had been squatting in Eastern District for a couple of years because one judge had recused himself, and it took an eternity for the new "Her Honor" to be appointed to the job. The pleading was a Rule 56 motion to dismiss Tubby's client's case on summary judgment. He didn't want to read it. Mercifully, Flowers showed up.

Cherrylynn ushered him in like he was royalty.

"Thank you, ma'am," he told her. "How are you, Tubby?" The detective appeared bright and eager, as always.

"Breaking up with my Florida girlfriend, I think. How are you?"

Tubby's loss didn't faze Flowers. "Hard at work. Do you want to hear about Caponata or the police union boss first?"

"You choose."

"They are related. Your police association president is Archie Alonzo, an important citizen, as you would expect. He rides in Bacchus. His wife filed for divorce on the basis that he chained her up on her birthday, which he characterized as 'rough love.' Apparently, she came around to his way of thinking. She dismissed the suit, and they seem to have reconciled. He was on the last mayor's transition team. The interesting thing is that he lives way beyond his means. His salary is about a hundred and fifty, but he's been going to Vail and to Grand Targhee Resort in the Tetons. He drives a Lexus LS, which costs close to $75,000. And he had a big ol' house in Tall Timbers. Estimated on Zillow to be worth more than a million. So he's got to be on the take somehow."

"All very interesting, but it doesn't get me closer to a defense for my errant police officer, Ireanous Babineaux."

"Right, well, this might possibly help. One of Alonzo's close friends is Trey Caponata. They've appeared together in the *Times-Picayune* society page. Both support the Kenner Rotary's efforts to curb cancer. And Caponata submitted an affidavit for Mister Alonzo, the union boss, in his divorce proceeding, before Alonzo's wife withdrew her petition. In the affidavit, Caponata, the mobster said that the union dude was a faithful member of the Saint Bonnabel School's dad's club, that he was known for his fried turkeys at Thanksgiving, that his wife was an exaggerator, even in high school, and that he had never seen any hint of marital discord between the two."

Tubby leaned forward with a grin on his face.

"This is pretty good stuff, detective. You mean to tell me that this wise guy Caponata, whose bodyguard is my client Ireanous Babineaux, is a bosom friend of Archie Alonzo, the man my client punched out?"

"Seems to be the case."

"Well, *embrasse moi tchew*, they're all in something together."

"No doubt about it."

"So, what do you think Caponata is into?"

"He's remarkably clean," the detective reported. "He supports the governor with money, but modestly, like five hundred here and there. Caponata has a girlfriend in Houston, but he keeps it quiet and has been married to the same woman for twenty years. No recent criminal record."

"Something is going on. I need to have a heart-to-heart with my client, Officer Babineaux."

"Shall I keep digging?"

"No. That's enough for now. But I would like you to check out someone else."

Flowers took out his iPad.

"He's Carlos Pancera. Who is this guy?"

Flowers stopped typing.

"He's not a secret, Tubby. That individual is a prominent citizen."

"You're kidding me. Who the hell is he?"

"He's the leader of the free-Cuba people here. All the Latinos get his email blasts, unless they block him out. His Facebook following is huge. He's been preaching about Castro since before I was born."

"Castro is still alive?"

Flowers frowned at him.

Tubby ignored him. "How come I don't know these people?" he complained.

"Maybe you are just not very involved in the Latino community, Tubby. But Pancera is an icon."

Chastening information. "I can't be in touch with everything," he said, recovering. "How old is he?"

"Maybe sixty, still going strong."

"What do you think his politics were in the 1970's?"

"Probably the same as today. Free Cuba. Nuke the commies."

"What about opening the dialogue? Cultural exchanges? Economic opportunities?"

Flowers laughed. "I don't think you appreciate the depths

of passion these folks have. Fortunately, New Orleans is just a sideshow. Their real influence is in Miami."

Maybe, or maybe not, Tubby thought. He asked Flowers to get some current information on Pancera.

XVI

When lunchtime rolled around, Tubby decided to take a stroll. The sky was clear and the weather was surprisingly pleasant, so he was willing to depart his Place Palais high-rise in the Central Business District and hike a few blocks just for the exercise. To the Contemporary Arts Center, in fact, where he hoped he might run into a certain volunteer. At the very least he might find an interesting exhibit that could serve, in a social situation, as a proper conversation starter.

The three-story brick edifice on Camp Street had once been the headquarters of the Katz and Besthoff drugstore chain, and memories of K&B's signature purple color, splashed on signs and logos and labels for treasured house brands such as Creole cream cheese ice cream at 89 cents a gallon and four-year-old bourbon for $4.25, still warmed the hearts of New Orleaneans over the age of 21.

Happily, the arts gallery was open. Actually, there was no one inside the expansive room, and Tubby strolled about, admiring this and that and trying to understand an exhibit of found-art sculpture, mostly constructed of re-purposed galvanized pipes and plumbing fixtures. Hung from the pipes, or in frames welded onto the arrangements, were photographs of "old" New Orleans, Mardi Gras, ballrooms, fruit vendors. The artist was identified as Dinky Bacon, the exhibitionist whose fund-raiser the lawyer had attended. Bacon was described on a placard as living in Rudduck, Louisiana.

As far as Tubby knew Rudduck was a boat-launch on the muddy banks of Lake Maurepas and anyone there would have to live in a shack accessible only by boating across narrow bayous overhung with Spanish moss and teeming with alligators and other reptiles. However did this artist get his works, some of which were quite bulky and cumbersome, in and out of a waterbound cabin in Rudduck? This question intrigued him more than the sculptures themselves.

"Are you a member, sir?" An elfin silken-haired girl with tattooed legs appeared at his side.

"No, not for years. Do I need to pay something?"

"It's actually ten dollars, but an annual membership costs only thirty-five and you get all sorts of special rates and invitations for the performing arts and our important events. We're just about to start the fall season."

"I'll be glad to pick up some information. Here's a ten. I was wondering if a woman who volunteers here, Peggy O'Flarity, might be around today."

"Ms. O'Flarity? Yes, I believe she's at the board meeting upstairs. They should be breaking up soon. Then they all have lunch."

"Ah. Would it be possible to give her a note?"

Apparently he looked respectable enough. "I could try," she said.

Hurriedly Tubby scribbled on the back of a business card. "Would you possibly like to have lunch with me? I'm downstairs now."

The girl looked at the note while pretending not to, and told him to stay put.

Tubby did. The gallery had floor-to-ceiling windows facing the street, and with that urban scenery as a background, the plumbing art, together with the antique photographs positioned at odd joints, gained a context. The lawyer went groping for insightful things to say to demonstrate his intellectual side.

Hearing the click of heels above, he looked up.

He was transfixed by a pair of legs in black shoes coming down the circular stairs.

"Mister Dubonnet. Is that right?" she asked when she had completed the spiral. She had a wide smile and twinkling blue eyes.

He found his voice and rose to the occasion. "You're saying it exactly right, but please call me Tubby. I was just in the neighborhood."

She took his hand and gave him a smile. "And I was just finishing a meeting. What do you think of our exhibit?"

"I think, as seen with the street as a backdrop, these works fit into our urban context."

Peggy O'Flarity had to suppress a laugh. "Well put," she said. "I can't wait to tell the artist. His show, however, is entitled 'Country Living.'"

"What does he know?"

"Quite right," Peggy agreed. "Did you invite me to lunch?"

"I certainly did. I'm afraid I don't have reservations. But we're close to Tivoli & Lee. I've never been there. Want to try it?"

"In the Hotel Modern, or Moderne, however you say it?"

"Yeah, it's just a couple of blocks."

"That would suit me, though I'm missing out on pizza and pasta salad with the rest of the board."

Tubby ushered her to the door. "You didn't tell me you were a board member." He took her elbow at the steps.

"Yes, and I have been for a couple of years. It's really a very important group."

Tubby was something of a stranger to non-profit boards.

He had always shied away from activities with no potential economic benefits other than fishing and hunting ducks.

"I'd like to hear more about your impressive group," he lied. "How does membership here compare to, say, being on the board of the New Orleans Art Museum, or the Ogden, or the Confederate Art Museum?"

She launched into a long and informed answer to that question.

He enjoyed the sound of her voice. He would have called it languid and sexy. She was learned. She dressed a lot smarter than he did. A white blouse, unbuttoned to a daring point, a bold, beaded necklace he thought could be lapis, a wide red belt, a sharp black skirt, and those heels.

He realized she had said something that he was supposed to respond to, but they had arrived at the restaurant. "Here we are," he said with relief.

"Oh, how nice and cool in here," she said. The first thing that met the eye was the bar, with colorful stools against one wall, and the second thing was the cheerful hostess who said that a table for two for lunch would be no problem.

She pointed at a little shiny table with stainless-steel chairs, but Tubby pointed to a booth upholstered in burgundy leather and said that's where they chose to be seated. They were given black napkins and spring water, and made quick work of ordering.

Peggy said she was sticking to her diet, and had a luncheon salad made of arugula and apples.

Tubby couldn't go quite that far, even for good health, so he ordered the Tivoli Burger, made from pedigreed beef topped with roasted garlic cream cheese, pepper jelly, pickled onions, and bacon. And, just to see how it would come out, an order of deviled eggs on the side.

"How about a glass of wine?" he suggested.

"Why not?" she said agreeably, and they each ordered a glass of Foxglove Chardonnay, maybe not fancy, but the best they had.

The establishment also offered a seventy-five-cent martini, but Tubby dismissed that as gauche under first-date circumstances.

"Was finding you today at the CAC my lucky break?" he asked. "Or do you come into the city often?"

As she began to speak, the most amazing thing happened. Her subject evolved into New Orleans, what she loved about it, what she hated about it, and he found himself totally engaged in her comments. She would make an observation about the architecture and the oak trees, and he would immediately have an impression of his own to share. The Lake, the history of the French Quarter, all the good things that had happened since Katrina. He was there. It had been a long time, about five years in fact, since he had had an actual conversation with an interesting and accomplished person who liked him. Talking to Raisin didn't count.

The food came. Tubby's burger in its warm bun was suitably immense. The deviled eggs, served on a square pearly dish, were each topped with a scoop of smoked gulf fish in a mousse and with a spoonful of big crispy capers. They each reached for one.

But the food was almost an afterthought. A good meal, they both said so, but they kept on talking. It had possibly been a long time for her, too.

Dessert menus arrived, and they both said no. But they ordered cappuccino while she described the Northshore—a land to which Tubby had seldom traveled. It had always represented, to him, a suburban wasteland occupied by narrow-minded, unfortunate people who had to commute hours each day, but she made it sound interesting. What with the beautiful farms, the trails, the rivers, the bicycling, and the cultural events in Covington.

"I'd sure like to explore it someday," he said, totally in her spell.

"You could if you like. Come on over and see my place. You can ride a horse."

They made a date for Saturday afternoon. She lived off Route 40, near Folsom.

* * *

After lunch they walked back to her parking spot near the Contemporary Arts Center, where they said goodbye. Strolling alone down Camp Street, Tubby was mentally flying, and he imagined how nice it would be to spend the rest of the afternoon out on the lake on his boat. That was way too complicated to make happen, however, since the boat, Lost Lady II, was on a trailer in his driveway and probably out of gas. He considered dropping over to his old bar, Mike's, on Annunciation Street in the Irish Channel. His Camaro, however, was parked at his office building, so that's where he ended up.

Once there, his mind inevitably shifted back to work. Cherrylynn gave him some messages, but nothing was as vexing as his lack of understanding of his police officer client, Ireanous Babineaux, and his apparent involvement with not just the union boss he had slugged but also with the mobster scion, Trey Caponata.

* * *

It took two or three tries, and in the intervals Tubby read a motion to dismiss his federal case—a motion he considered repetitive and frivolous—but finally Babineaux called back.

"Have you heard anything further about Archie Alonzo, the guy you hit, bringing up any charges?" the lawyer asked.

"The word is out he's going to charge me," Babineaux said, "but I haven't seen anything so far."

"You told me he provoked you. Were there any witnesses to that?"

"Yeah, Rick Sandoval. He'll say I was provoked."

"By touching your chest with his finger?"

"That's right."

"Did anyone else see this? I mean, Sandoval and you worked together and might be seen as friends. Were there angry words? Did anyone else hear them?"

"The only other person in the room was Alonzo's suck-up vice president, and he'll say whatever his boss tells him to say."

"Got it. What was the argument about?"

"I told you. Alonzo didn't like me operating the off-duty officer job referral service. He wanted it all for himself, so to speak."

"You told me that your so-called service was being replaced by an official central dispatch for the whole department."

"Yeah, but under the union contract, that dispatch is operated by the police benevolent association, which is run by Alonzo. It takes a percentage, and that ends up in Alonzo's pocket."

"That makes things a lot more clear. I didn't understand that Alonzo had a personal interest in cancelling out your deal. But tell me, how did Sandoval happen to be there when the argument broke out?"

"Rick was my partner in the business. You need a black guy

and a white guy for everything in New Orleans. I'm the black guy. He's my white guy. That's the way it is."

"That's the way it is?"

"That's the way it is."

"How did you get to know Sandoval?"

"We actually injured each other in high school. I was playing for St. Augustine and he was playing for Jesuit. He tackled me and broke my collarbone. I rolled over on him and broke his ankle. We were both in casts for the rest of the season, making faces at each other from the sidelines."

"How did Trey Caponata become a part of your arrangement, or was he a part?"

After a pause, Babineaux asked, "What makes you want to know that?"

"It's an odd coincidence that you worked for Caponata, and that Caponata is a good friend of Alonzo. You didn't tell me that Caponata and your victim were such good friends."

"Once upon a time we was all good friends."

"Not anymore?"

"Trey is siding with me for right now. He and I go way back together, too. I've saved him from getting into a lot of shit he couldn't handle."

"I see."

"What do you see?"

"I see you may have been covering up for a criminal."

"Trey is legit."

"Then he's the first Caponata that is."

Babineaux didn't respond. He wasn't giving anything up.

"I'm just wondering," Tubby said, leaning back from his desk as if the client were actually in the room, "might there not be a business solution to this whole thing?"

"What's that mean, 'business solution'?"

"Maybe I don't have a full enough appreciation of what

your business was, or is, but in general terms it sounds like you and President Alonzo are fighting over a particular pot of money, and Caponata, whatever his relationship to this business might be, has ties to you both. Like I say, in big-picture terms, I'm wondering if there might not be a dollars-and-cents solution that could be worked out among all concerned."

"Not while that prick Alonzo has me working over in the Fifth District. I think he wants to get me shot."

"Tempers are high," Tubby said. "But maybe it's a good time to offer a compromise. After all, you got in a pretty good punch."

"He has pins in his jaw," Ireanous said with satisfaction.

"Give it some thought," Tubby counseled. "Time heals all wounds. You say you haven't received a hearing date for your grievance?"

"No. Not a peep."

"I could call someone and see what's happening."

"No. I'm not sure what having an attorney butt in right now would get me. They might want to shuffle this whole thing under the rug."

"That's what you hope?"

"I guess I do. I need to get Internal Affairs out of this so that I can make my own arrangements. But I do want to have you in the wings for when I need you."

"Think about what I said. Maybe there's a business solution."

"I will. Listen, if I get out of this shit hole transfer, maybe I can get your quality of life officer Jane Smith sent somewhere far away, too."

"I wouldn't want you to impact her career negatively."

"What career?" Babineaux spat out. "The Fifth District is a dumping ground. Officer Smith is only here because she got in trouble for dating our chief's daughter."

"No! She's gay?"

"Call it what you want. But from what I heard, Smith wouldn't put a ring on it, so she fell out of favor."

"Your police department sounds like some old-world duchy or Russian oligarchy…"

"You lost me. I gotta go."

Tubby could hear the policeman's radio squawking in the background.

The connection broke.

XVII

"What's some lawyer named Tubby Dubonnet doing screwing around in my business?" Carlos Pancera demanded.

He had Jason Boaz pinned down in a small office in the basement of a church.

"What? Who?" Jason fumbled for an answer. Carlos and his moral rectitude had always intimidated him.

"He's your lawyer, isn't he?" Pancera yelled. "I've heard about that for years. You want some coffee?"

"Yes, please," Jason said.

Carlos rang a bell and a pretty brown-skinned girl, who couldn't have been more than fifteen, entered from behind a curtain.

"Bring us each a coffee," Pancera told her and she disappeared.

"I got a call from a policeman I know," Pancera resumed. "Your lawyer is inquiring about me in connection with a shooting that happened to some nameless hippie decades ago. Decades ago! What's all that about?"

"Carlos, you may remember…"

"I remember nothing. What do you remember?"

"Nothing," Jason said helplessly. "I wasn't there."

"You were one of us then. You came from a good family. What happened to you?"

"I make substantial contributions every year. Leave me alone." Boaz was defending himself.

Pancera held up both palms to stop such nonsense. "You've drifted away from us."

"I don't remember Cuba," Jason whined. "I have never met a Communist. I have other concerns that are far more important to me."

"Like what? Global warming?"

"Actually, yes. Coastal subsidence is another one. Did you know that the Louisiana coastline is disappearing at the rate of a football field an hour…?"

"Oh, shut up!" Pancera thundered. "Your family's home, your inheritance, was stolen by a filthy maniac who is still a dictator and the champion of world-wide socialism. His cancerous ideas are still taking root every day right here in the United States."

"But there are other threats today, my friend Pancera. Disease. Radical Islam. Overpopulation. Rising seas."

"You are starting to sound like a fucking socialist yourself. That could always lead to a sudden death. The future of freedom, capitalism, and family values is ours to shape, to take. You must come back to us and do your share."

"I am doing my share," Jason protested, shaken by the reference to a sudden death. "I have given the benevolent society and the veterans of the Brigade almost a hundred thousand dollars over the years."

"*No puede haber paz sin justicia.* Do you remember what happened to 'Second-in-Command'?"

Jason was confused. "I remember hearing he drowned in Katrina."

"Yeah, but he had some help. Don't you know that the Night Watchman got him?"

"No!" Jason was shocked. "All that rough stuff was supposed to be over years ago."

Pancera stared at him with black eyes that didn't blink.

"What was his offense?" Jason asked.

"He tried to destroy 'the papers.'"

Jason dimly recalled mentions of 'the papers' decades before, but he denied it now. "I don't know anything about any papers," he said. "I just want peace. What are you asking me to do?"

"Get this lawyer Dubonnet off my case. *Dejar morir muertos en paz.*"

"How can I let the dead lie in peace, tell me?"

"You will find a way. You have always been a very smart fellow, Jason. There are many others involved in this, as you know. They do not want their lives to be disturbed by ancient events. They move very fast when they are threatened. Make this go away. You got it?" His fingers did little dances like snowflakes falling. "Just make it go away. Or else we will act as we must."

* * *

"Mr. Boaz is on the phone," Cherrylynn called from the other room.

"Hi, Jason. What's up?"

"All the stuff we talked about, I can't talk about, but I want to say, you know, we're friends."

"Okay," Tubby said encouragingly.

"And I've finished my little decibel invention. I think it will suit your purposes admirably."

"Great. Great. You didn't have to. Like you said, I can probably buy one at the store. But, of course, I'd like to have yours."

"You absolutely should. Mine's better. You can field-test it for me and see how well it works."

"Gladly."

"I can drop it off at your home tonight."

"That works. I'm leaving here soon. I have to stop at the grocery store and pick up some stuff, but I should be home by six."

"No problem. I'll see you then."

After hanging up Tubby stared for a minute at the life of his city beyond his office window. Far off in the east there was a plume of smoke, maybe a house on fire. He could see a traffic jam building up on the I-10. Sounds of a brass band rose up from Bourbon Street, forty-three stories below. There was a very large bird circling over the panorama, flying even higher than Tubby's office. Likely it was a bald eagle whose nest was at Bayou Sauvage, coming back from its daily feast in the Gulf of Mexico. Burning buildings, snags on the Interstate, vast distances, meant nothing to that extraordinary creature.

Maybe, he thought, when I solve the Parker murder, when Collette finishes school, when I find the right woman, I can be free like that.

Nah! A fantasy. He collected his briefcase and headed out the door.

* * *

Tubby was steering his handsome Camaro uptown on Magazine Street when Raisin caught up with him on the mobile.

"Want to go out tonight? Janie's bar?"

"That's what you say every night, but I can't. No point in it till I get my noise meter. Jason is bringing it over in an hour. Let's go tomorrow."

"Does all of this noise pollution crap sound like nannyville to you?" Raisin wanted to know. "Didn't we use to stand right next to the speakers at Grateful Dead, the Band, Aerosmith, Led Zeppelin, Janice Joplin? Didn't the whole floor vibrate?"

"I can't hear you."

"But really, hasn't the music always been loud? Remember Benny's on Camp?"

"Oh, man, yes. At two in the morning you could hear it all the way down to Napoleon Avenue."

"And nobody thought there was anything wrong with that."

"Well, maybe the neighbors did."

"I doubt it. The neighbors then were a lot younger and hipper. Everybody thought local music was cool. That was the sound of New Orleans! I mean the Nevilles lived two blocks away. Everything in those days was less uptight, less high class."

"Well, Raisin, we can still see the Wild Tchoupitoulas and the Buzzards on Valence Street," Tubby said.

"Less and less often."

"You think?"

"Take the Bywater," his friend said. "It used to be just trains, working people and lead paint. When did they start caring about how loud the music was?"

"I don't really know. Neighborhoods change."

"I'm going to the bar by myself. I want some action."

"Why not knock on a few of the neighbors' doors while you're over there and see if anyone is really bothered by the noise?"

"I might just do that. What the F-bomb."

"Is that what we've come to? And you are a guy who knows what a real bomb is."

"The times are way too mellow now, Tubby."

* * *

With his feet up on the glass coffee table in his living room, Tubby Dubonnet was reading a history of Andrew Jackson's Indian wars and sipping a toddy. The doorbell rang. Reluctantly, he got up and let Jason in.

"How about a drink," he offered.

"No," Jason said. He seemed very agitated. He was carrying a rectangular black briefcase with brass clasps. "Let's just sit down."

They did, in the living room, on two chairs separated by the coffee table. Tubby had furnished his place slowly over the years. It was still sparse and simple, featuring lighter woods like cypress and pine, despite advice from his daughters and various girlfriends who seemed to prefer things solid and dark.

Jason opened his briefcase on the table and extracted a 9mm automatic pistol, also black, which he pointed in the area of Tubby's knee.

"I am supposed to threaten you with this to make you stop asking questions about things that happened when we were young. And I'm supposed to shoot you if I fail."

Tubby's eyes didn't leave the gun.

"But you know me." Jason waved the pistol in the air as Tubby's gaze followed it. "That's not my nature. So, no. I can't do it!" He re-stowed the weapon very neatly in his briefcase.

"Here is what I prefer to do. I want to give you a legal fee of fifty thousand dollars, and you will represent me until I die or go crazy, and you will stop all these inquiries."

Tubby shook his head to clear it and took a deep breath.

"Are you offering me a fifty-thousand-dollar bribe?" he asked.

"To me it is a legal fee," Boaz said. "Believe me, I have the money."

"I don't know if I believe you or not, but what makes you think..."

"Tubby," Jason pressed his hands together as if in prayer. His bearded chin bobbed up and down and his black glasses jiggled, "that shows how important this is to me. It may be a matter of my life or death." He touched his heart. "And I know you could use the money. Who couldn't? And it would solve everything. I'm desperate."

"No." Tubby stood up. He was looking for an opportunity to snatch the briefcase, but Jason hastily drew it into his lap and popped the clasps open.

Tubby had a gun of his own in the house, but unfortunately it was upstairs in the nightstand by his bed.

"I was afraid you would say that, my friend, and you might as well have signed a death warrant. But, hell, Tubby. That's just the way you are, right? You never were a crooked man." His tone changed back to friendly. "I suppose we must just let the chips fall where they may. *A pesar de las consecuencias*, as they say in the old country. It may all work out. This is the twenty-first century after all, not the 1970s. I'll give you my special device anyway. Come sit by me." He indicated the sofa, where Tubby's book still lay, spread open to the page he had been enjoying.

"I'll stand, thank you," Tubby said warily.

"Okay, but my invention is not so big." Boaz pulled a mobile phone from his case. "The screen will be hard for you to see."

"Don't worry about it," Tubby said.

"This is a new Samsung I just bought, and I programed it with this very ingenious app I invented. Here's what you can do." He clicked it on. "Now, speak loudly."

"You are an extremely bad client!" Tubby said with considerable volume, while Jason aimed the phone at him.

"Excellent," the inventor said. "Now let's see what you can replay here." He did some scrolling around and then held up the screen for Tubby to see.

He beheld himself, a chest and head shot, with his Rodrigue print hanging behind him on the wall, nervously yelling, "You are an extremely bad client."

Jason demonstrated with his finger that today's date and time, and a running count of the decibel level, all appeared below the video. Tubby's voice had measured from 60 to 75 decibels.

"It's very simple," Jason said proudly. He gave the device to Tubby.

"That's the way it works. That's the only thing it does. Use it in good health."

The visitor latched his case and stood up.

"I feel quite a relief," he said. "I have neither shot you nor spent fifty thousand dollars."

He made his way to the door quickly, with Tubby close behind him.

"If I live through all this," Boaz continued, "maybe I will make some money from this invention."

Tubby let him out and promptly double-locked the door.

He tossed the phone on the chair and went directly into his kitchen for something straight and serious.

"Christ," he said out loud. "This town is completely full of insane people."

XVIII

Raisin had put away a few at the bar. Feeling bulletproof, he thought he might just prowl around the neighborhood and be friendly, so he went outside.

Right next door to Janie's club was a shotgun house with a hand-painted sign outside that said "KEEP OFF STEPS. CLEAN UP DOG MESS." On the curb in front of the house were a pair of homemade "NO PARKING" signs stuck in paint cans that had been filled with cement. Raisin had noticed these when he arrived and obligingly had parked in front of an adjacent empty lot. Certainly this was a promising house if one were looking for prickly neighbors.

He rapped on the glass pane of the front door. In a moment the door cracked open a few inches, constrained by a safety chain.

"What you want?" The man inside was a stocky African-American in a T-shirt. His round head was bald except for a fringe of white hair.

"No problem," said Raisin. "I'm asking about the bar next door. I heard there were complaints about the loud music."

"What's it to you?"

"I'm a friend of the owner," Raisin said. "I'd like to see what can be done to make the situation better."

"Y'all can clear out of this neighborhood. That would make the situation a whole lot better."

"I'm not sure who this 'y'all' is, but…"

"All you rich honkies think you can run over people who've been here all their lives."

"Hey, do I look white to you?"

The man tried to see better through the crack. It was dark outside.

"Not too sure," he admitted.

"I am of French extraction, primarily. Maybe some Creole. But what's the deal? Half the musicians who play at that bar are black."

"I don't care if they are. I don't care for that music."

"Tell the truth, I don't either."

"It rattles my walls."

"What do you do at night?"

"What do you do? I try to sleep."

"You work during the day?"

"I was a longshoreman at the Louisa Street wharf for twenty-four years."

"But you don't work now, so you can get up late in the morning if you want to."

"I don't want to."

"You can have a belt or two at night if you want to."

"What's a belt?"

"A shot. A hit off the bottle. A Jack and Coke."

"I could if I wanted to."

"Let's have a belt."

"I ain't got Jack. Maybe some Coke, but I don't keep whiskey in the house."

"No worries, babe. I got a bottle right here in my car. What if I bring it in the house and we just sit down and savor?"

"Maybe." The man was interested.

Raisin's car, the red Miata, was only a few yards away. He fetched his load from the trunk where it was stored judiciously out of the driver's compartment.

"Sorry, dude," he called over his shoulder. "It isn't Jack Daniel's. It's Maker's Mark." He displayed the red-capped bottle.

The homeowner opened the door and waved him inside.

"My name's Raisin."

"Monk. Ashton Monk. Come on back."

They went through the man's living room, full of old furniture and with pictures of Jesus, JFK, Robert, and MLK on the mantle. And through the bedroom and another bedroom, to the kitchen.

"Pardon all this mess. I'm a bachelor. Take a chair. I've got some glasses somewhere."

XIX

It was a Code 10-30, a burglary in process.

"This is what we live for," Ireanous Babineaux said to himself. To the dispatcher he said, "Five-O-Six, on it."

"Unit Seven-O-One and Four Ten, are you responding?" was the dispatcher's dry question.

Babineaux killed the radio when he was a block away, and snapped off his lights.

Cruise in swiftly and silently. Double-park outside the shuttered furniture store on Chartres Street.

Probably a false alarm. Not much to steal here. He relaxed.

On the other side of the levee, a docked container ship's tall sparkling towers gave more illumination to the street than the city lights did. It was a nondescript old-time store with dark alleys on either side. Somewhere in the back of the store an alarm was ringing. No one was on the street. The other cars hadn't come yet.

Babineaux heard someone or something scrambling about in the back alley. It sounded to him like the perps were trying to get away over a fence. His instincts to catch the bad guy overtook his good sense.

"Give it up! Police!" he cried and took one step into the darkness.

Two shots cracked out, but he only heard the first one, the one that put a hole in his forehead.

Footsteps peppered down the sidewalk. A car started on the next block. A ship sounded its horn. Lights out, another police cruiser crept down the street, while Babineaux's life slipped away.

* * *

The downed policeman's Glock lay beside his outstretched hand on the pavement. The safety was still on. That's what the responding officer, Victor Argueta, noticed first. He had the alley cordoned off with yellow tape, and they brought out some lights. No sign of forced entry in any of the buildings in the immediate vicinity.

Since the coroner was on his way, the detective crossed the street and sat down on the grass of the levee. He popped some Wrigley's spearmint and wished he was still allowed to smoke cigarettes on the job. It was peaceful and airy over here, across the street and ten yards away from the violence and the spotlights. Crickets chirped in the grass. His pants felt the damp. This scene didn't make sense. Why did the cop go down that alley alone? That dismal, full-of-garbage, empty alley? Was he an idiot?

* * *

Tubby found out about the shooting by reading the newspaper the next morning, and he immediately called Flowers.

"It couldn't have been Caponata," Flowers said. "He was at the Hot Pockets Casino in Biloxi watching women's boxing until 5 o'clock this morning."

"Who is working the Babineaux shooting?"

"I'll find out."

"The lid is on this investigation," Flowers reported a few minutes later. "There is no particular detective assigned to it. A cop named Victor Argueta was on the scene, but it's not officially his file. Internal Affairs has a piece of it, which means everybody else stands back. That's what I'm hearing. I'm afraid my connections in that particular department are limited, but I'm working on it."

"We have to figure this out," Tubby protested. "He was my client."

"I'll keep looking," Flowers promised. "Oh, here's another bit. They're also looking into another cop in that district. She's one Jane Smith."

"The quality of life officer?"

"You are right, sir. How'd you know?"

"It is tempting and very frustrating to imagine connections everywhere and not have the slightest clue what those connections might be."

"No comment, boss. I'll call you if…"

"…I have anything," they both said at once.

* * *

Officer Sandoval was on the phone with Tubby.

"Did you hear about Babineaux?" the cop asked.

"Yes," Tubby said. "Tough break."

"Real tough."

"I'm really sorry about it. I don't even know how it happened."

"I hear he went into a dark alley by himself," Sandoval said. "Which he shouldn't have done. He's no rookie, but that's the kind of guy he was."

"What do you mean?"

"A macho guy. A crime fighter."

"Have they caught the shooter?"

"No. I want to meet with you in person."

"Sure. Absolutely. When?"

"Right now would be good."

"I can do that."

"Le Bon Temps Roulé uptown. Know where that is?

"Sure. Are you allowed?"

"Today's my day off. I'm not in uniform."

"I can be there in about fifteen minutes."

"I'm already here."

* * *

Le Bon Temps Roulé was a venerable neighborhood dive on Magazine Street with a pool table and a piano. It was open all the time, though early morning customers had to lift their shoes to let Jessie Beach do his daily mopping. The bar's jukebox never stopped, so at a table by the window Tubby's and Sandoval's conversation was hidden by "Help Me, Rhonda," followed by the Ventures, which someone who had already caught a cab had selected. The volume wasn't at maximum, since it was late morning. The barmaid left them alone.

"Quite a while since I've been here," Tubby mused. He was searching for the Moss Man photo that used to hang over the portal to the back bar. "Are we drinking?" he asked.

"I don't drink," Sandoval said. He looked like he'd been working out for a couple of hours. His white T-shirt stretched to cover his major biceps. He had on navy-blue sweat pants below.

"It's a little early for me, too," Tubby said regretfully. They were now the only patrons in the place.

"Sorry about your partner," Tubby said again.

"My partner?"

"Babineaux. He said you ran the off-duty officer thing together."

"He always talked too much."

Tubby shrugged.

Sandoval said, "He told me he hired you to be his lawyer."

"That's true, but his check hasn't cleared."

"It will. Babineaux was usually straight with the money." Sandoval lowered his big head for a moment, as if in silent prayer. His eyes might have been moist. "Bad stomach," he said, recovering.

"Did he leave a family?" Tubby asked.

"He's got a kid up north who will probably get his benefits, little as he deserves them, and a girlfriend on Transcontinental who could use the money. We'll probably pass the hat to help her out."

"What do you think happened to him?"

"What did he hire you to do?"

"That's a professional, what do you say, confidence, but it basically deals with the dustup with your union president, Archie Alonzo."

"Was that all he wanted to talk about?"

"I can't tell you more than I just said."

"Well, what do you know about Alonzo?"

"Only what Ireanous told me, and I can't share that with you."

"Then if you won't talk, you can't help me," Sandoval said, with an unpleasant snort. "And sticking your nose where it doesn't belong didn't help Babineaux."

"Who says I was sticking my nose anywhere?"

"I do. Archie Alonzo does."

"Did Alonzo set Babineaux up?"

"Not in person." Sandoval seemed disappointed. "Alonzo

was at some meeting with the mayor. I think some hood off the street blew Babineaux away. But by Alonzo just sending a crime-buster like Ireanous into a crime-ridden neighborhood— it was like sending him to the executioner. Everybody knew that. It was to be expected."

"I heard he was shot at close range with his safety still on." Tubby had gotten that from Flowers, who had gotten it from a detective Argueta.

"Really?" Sandoval said. "Then it must have happened fast."

"Yeah."

"That's that," Sandoval said. "You're not telling me anything new about my old partner, and I'm out of here."

"Wait!" Tubby got a grip on the cop's forearm. "Weren't you and Ireanous close?"

"In what way?" the cop asked. "We weren't married."

"You were friends in school."

"We beat the shit out of each other in high school."

"Was Trey Caponata part of your business deal?"

"Caponata tries to be a part of everybody's deal. He comes up with a lot of jobs for our off-duty cops, like Italian weddings and graduations. But he's the kind of a guy who always needs a little slice for himself." The policeman pulled away from Tubby's grip.

"Where does this leave you?" Tubby asked. "Are you going to keep working in Police Records?"

"Don't you worry about me, Dubonnet. I'll take care of myself. And it seems to me that you don't have any more business in police affairs."

"You can call me if you need any legal advice," Tubby told him.

"I'll take care of myself," Sandoval said again. He pushed himself out of the booth and walked out of the bar.

Tubby watched him get into his police car and scratch off from the curb. The street was empty except for the vapors rising from the outdoor smoker of a barbeque joint across the street. A passing city bus blew them away. Tubby leaned back and closed his eyes to think.

He wondered absently how Sandoval knew that the police union boss Alonzo had been at a meeting with the mayor when Babineaux was shot. He wondered what Sandoval had hoped to learn from him in the first place.

The cop's departure brought the bartender back to life.

"Want anything, sweetie?" she called from the bar.

Tubby shook his head.

He felt that he needed to go home and take a shower.

XX

"Ms. Peggy O'Flarity gave me your name," the voice on the phone began. That was an introduction that worked.

"How can I help you?"

"I go by the name of Dinky Bacon, Mr. Dubonnet, and I am a visceral artist."

"Ah, are you the gentleman who was arrested for being naked in Jackson Square?" Tubby had known this call was inevitable from his first encounter with Peggy, bless her heart.

"That is hardly the extent of my artistic presentation, but nudity in front of the cliché of Saint Louis Cathedral, where every crying child in America has been photographed by its mother, and the grit of street people who surround that religious edifice, goes to the substance of my art, which in my estimation…"

"I'm sure that's true," Tubby interrupted. "I've also seen some of your plumbing sculpture at the Contemporary Arts Center. But, Mister Bacon, where are you calling from?"

"I'm in the parish jail."

"I thought they raised your bail money last week at the benefit concert."

"They did, but would you believe there was a detainer out for me for failing to appear in court last November?"

"What was that charge all about?"

"Art and nudity at the Voodoo Fest. I duct-taped myself to one of Drake's speakers. All they gave me that time was a ticket."

"Yet you didn't appear?"

"That's what they say."

"Is your time on this phone limited?"

"Yes, sir, it is. There is a line of criminals waiting for me to get off."

"Do you have a lawyer?"

"I thought I did. He was a volunteer, and a very nice young man, I thought, but after they said I couldn't go home, he left, and I haven't seen him again."

"Do you want a lawyer?"

"Yes, I think I need one, and Ms. O'Flarity said you were the very best."

It was hard not to cry.

"Got it. Do they have you booked under the name of Dinky Bacon?"

"No, my real name is on my wristband."

The lawyer sighed, and waited. Nothing more was forthcoming.

"What is the name on your wristband?" he finally asked.

"Tobias Magnum," the client said reluctantly.

"Well, too bad, Tobias. This is Friday. There are basically no judges around until Monday. Even if I found a judge and she was willing to release you on your own recognizance, there is no one at the jail with the authority to cut you loose this afternoon. In any case, I am going to be gone for the next couple of days, so whatever I might do will not happen over the weekend."

"I'm going to miss my sister's birthday."

"I'm just telling you my situation."

"I don't know anybody else to call."

"Neither do I. Public Defender?"

"They say next week."

"There you have it."

"But there will be a producer from the Arts Channel at my sister's birthday bash. He's coming to film me. It's my big break!" Bacon was distraught.

"Tell you what," Tubby said. "Give me the producer's name and number and I'll call him. I will tell him your plight, and maybe he'll see a story in it and come over to the jail with a film crew. Wouldn't that be the lead-up to a great documentary?"

"Man, it sure would. Wait. I've got his number memorized."

He rattled it off, and Tubby read it back to confirm. What sounded like a fight was breaking out around the jail pay phone, and the call ended.

Despite the gloomy picture he had painted for Dinky Bacon, the attorney decided to take a shot and called the Honorable Alvin Hughes, the one judge he knew who might be willing to do something on his holiday.

XXI

Saturday morning came up typical New Orleans beautiful, and Tubby was very grateful that he had been invited to take a trip to the country. He had promised to be at Peggy's on the Northshore at about 11:30. They would enjoy the air, take a tour, eat some lunch and, if he liked, go riding. He bounded out of bed at his normal 6:30 and donned a pair of new blue jeans and an expensive checkered skirt from the Orvis store in the Warehouse District.

His phone buzzed, and it was Raisin.

"I was out in Janie's neighborhood last night," he said.

"Can you tell me about it later?" Tubby asked. "I've got some important matters involving a lady I need to attend to."

"Okay. Did you get that sound meter from your bud?"

"Sure, I did." Tubby didn't go over the point where Boaz had threatened him with a gun.

"I'd like to fool around with it if you don't mind."

"Not at all. It's simple to operate. You just turn it on and point. Cherrylynn knows where it is, and she can figure out how to get it to you."

He wasn't sure how long it would take him to drive the fifty miles into the totally unfamiliar country of the far north. Like a lot of city dwellers, the lawyer simply never had any need to go across the lake. But he was psyched for this trip and he hit the road right after downing a single cup of coffee. First, a stop to fill up the gas tank at the Shell station by the river and check his tires and oil. Can't be too careful when you're on a long expedition across a vast body of water. Second, he pulled into Dot's Diner on Jefferson Highway, a favorite breakfast joint that he rarely visited because it was off his beat.

The special thing was, they were friendly. They also had several different morning papers lying around, and kept your coffee cup full. And they made their own biscuits. He took his time ordering and eating. The diner didn't sell booze, but there was a bar next door that advertised good Bloody Marys at an attractive price. He was immensely full of high-calorie food, however, so he abstained and rolled onto the highway.

The Lake Pontchartrain Causeway calls itself the longest bridge in the world, at 24 miles, though other bridge builders—in China and Turkey for instance—have challenged the claim. It is, however you measure it, inarguably long, and it crosses the wide, brackish inland sea that makes New Orleans almost an island. It provides an option for urban sprawlers who, if they don't mind the distance, can spread out into the rolling piney woods of St. Tammany Parish to create gated communities, Christian schools, and golf courses wherever they like. The drive to get to and from the Northshore gives thousands of daily commuters the opportunity to meditate, to explore books-on-tape, or to read all of their text messages while gazing over the long miles of blue crab trap floats running beside the bridge. They could stare at the distant white sailboats, cruising in the sun's glare and captained by people far more fortunate than the working stiffs behind the wheel.

The morning drive northward was opposite to the commuters' direction and therefore quite peaceful. There was a light chop in the lake. Its sparkling waters stretched to every horizon. The morning sun was off to the right, not blinding, but golden.

White birds searched for trout, and Tubby cranked up Chuck Berry singing "Johnny B. Goode" on WWOZ.

To get to Folsom, once off the bridge, you had to pass first through miles of strip malls and traffic lights, which gave drivers time to ponder questions like who might St. Tammany have been, until at last the Walmarts and subdivisions gave way to "Acreage For Sale" signs. Tubby realized that he was still running a bit early, so he poked along, even stopping at a fruit stand to encourage local food by buying some fresh honey. It would end up in his pantry back home with all the rest of his unopened jars of country honey, craft-fair chow-chow and mysterious jalapeno salsas.

He followed his MapQuest directions to a narrow blacktop road that wound around rolling pasturelands and past the occasional polo club. Tubby had never watched a polo match, but he knew it to be a pastime for the wealthy. Peggy O'Flarity's driveway was gravel, and he slowed to spare the paint job on his restored Camaro. A large split-level brick home surrounded by hedges and trees with bright flowers appeared, and his hostess was in a porch swing waiting. He suppressed the temptation to fishtail as he came around her circular drive.

"Here you are," she said happily, rising to greet him as he climbed out of his car.

He gave her the proper kiss on the cheek.

She offered Sangria from a pitcher afloat with orange slices, which he naturally accepted, though it wasn't his drink. He sat down on the porch rail facing her in the swing—all very much as he imagined a proper country squire would do. The sun was on his back. It lit up her face and brightened her white shirt with the sleeves rolled up.

"Are you hungry or would you like to see my place first?" she asked.

"I'd like to see your place. It's very nice to be out of the city."

"Isn't it? Coming here is just so invigorating. Do you smell the hay?"

"Yes, now that you mention it."

"They just cut it yesterday," she said proudly.

"How many horses do you have?"

"Only six. And one is too old to ride." He thought six was quite a large number.

"What do they all do?" he asked.

She smiled at the question. "Oh, I ride them. I also have friends who join me for what we call 'expeditions.' I have a groom who takes care of the stables and all that."

"Do you have a cook and a butler, too?"

"No," she laughed. "My horses are cared for far better than I am. I actually have to cook and dress myself." She was wearing jeans, with the white shirt, unbuttoned at the collar, and a substantial gold necklace with a green stone that fell about where the top button of her shirt would have been.

After they finished their beverages, she took him walking around the estate. They visited a hay barn, the stables, the head of a trail she said stretched for miles over the farms of the other landed gentry, and a spot she liked where you could look over a pond at a long green horizon of trees. She said it was a special place for sunsets. Then they went back to the house for lunch, Tubby nodding while she chatted away like a tour guide.

Lunch would be nothing fancy, she said. Just a lump crab salad with an aioli dressing made of garlic, olive oil, lemon juice and egg yolks, served on crispy tortillas, which she admitted she had made. He was quite bowled over, and he also appreciated her simply and tastefully furnished house. The furniture was contemporary. There was incredible art on the walls, oils, watercolors, photographs, and glass art pieces. They sat in the kitchen, and she served them more wine.

"What do you really do for a living?" she asked at one point.

"Mostly I represent people whom I find interesting and try to get the best possible results for them. I'm a problem solver."

"Are you an ethical lawyer?" she asked, coyly flashing her eyes at him.

"I never lie to the judge," Tubby said. "And I never screw a client. But I do try to get paid."

"That all sounds very sensible."

She cleared the plates into the sink, and he helped. They talked again on the porch, and he learned that she had gone to school at the University of Arkansas, where one of her daughters was now enrolled. Another daughter was about to get married in Nashville. The ex-husband, the attorney in New Orleans, was bending over backwards to pay for the wedding in ways too splendid to comprehend. Tubby was amazed that he didn't recognize the guy's name, but the fact was he didn't travel in the same circles as most of the big-firm guys.

"So would you like to go riding?" she asked.

Rashly, Tubby said yes. It will all come back to me, he thought. Apparently his willingness to have an adventure had been anticipated, because two of the horses were already saddled and waiting outside the barn.

"You won't want to push Ramses very hard," Peggy said. "He's getting so old and lazy."

"All the better." Tubby managed to mount without assistance. Peggy did so far more gracefully and she knew comforting words to whisper in her nag's ear.

They took off on a leisurely trot across a wide field, and Tubby found that a measure of his teenage horsemanship did come back. They followed a farm lane over the hills that had views of far-away mansions and miles of green pine trees. More than two hours passed this way, and the sun began to set. Tubby regretted that the day was ending and told her so. She had obviously enjoyed herself, too, so he took a chance.

"Can I take you out to dinner?" he asked.

"Tonight? You don't have to do that."

"But I want to if there's somewhere you like. Where do people eat around here?"

"There are a couple of choices."

"Do they sell wine?"

"Are you kidding? Even the gas stations around here have full bars. Gus's is the best food in Folsom, but it's mostly breakfast and po-boys. We're only a hop and a skip from Covington, and we could get a table at Del Porto or Ox Lot 9."

* * *

The meal at the Ox Lot, named for an earlier, more rustic period in the town's history, was over the top. They drank chicory-infused Manhattans and Premiere Cru Bordeaux, and they ate Oyster Patties, Whole Roasted Red Snapper, and Grilled Colorado Venison, which was prepared with the sort of things that make a chef's eyes sparkle, like rutabaga puree, roasted baby turnips, Tangipahoa Parish kale, beech mushrooms, and green pepper *jus*. Tubby was feeling pleasured beyond belief. Peggy was stroking his ankle with the pointy toe of her high heels. This restaurant was in an old and beautifully restored railside hotel, once the town's center, and Tubby was leaning closer to suggest that they get a room. But before he could pounce, she got a grip on herself and said, in a tone not to be argued with, that it was time to go home.

Almost always a gentleman, he steered them to his black muscle car, and they set off on the two-lane blacktop northward. They laughed most of the way while listening to greatest hits on the radio. He was proud of getting her home without incident, though he had some doubts whether he could sail through a sobriety test.

Pulling into her driveway, she asked, "Do you think you can make it back to New Orleans?"

"Oh, yeah," he proclaimed, before realizing it was a trick question. "Honestly, I do think I can. But would you like to do this again sometime?"

"I'd love to."

Peggy popped out of the car. "Let's see whether you can get out of the driveway."

As a matter of fact, he did very well, only flirting with the lawn twice.

"I should have handled that differently," Tubby told himself as he drove down the dark lonely road. But he was actually quite satisfied with the evening. Important groundwork had been laid. She wanted to see him again. The black sky was full of amazing stars. You couldn't see a show like this in the city.

These country people drive like maniacs, Tubby thought. There was a pick-up truck, or maybe a large SUV, racing from behind him. Tubby braced himself, afraid that he was going to get rear-ended. The crazy driver slowed just in time. He was prevented from passing by a sharp curve in the road and a double-yellow line and settled in a few yards behind the Camaro's rear bumper. Tubby drove erratically, almost blinded by the high-riding vehicle's blazing headlamps.

"What the hell!" he cursed. The blacktop straightened out and the truck could pass, but it hung onto Tubby's tail for another painful quarter-mile before suddenly pulling around. For a few seconds it travelled beside the Camaro, long enough for Tubby to see that he was aside a black Lincoln Navigator. Then the Navigator tried to force him off the highway into a ditch. Tubby swerved to avoid contact and floored it. The Camaro was old, but it was fast. The Lincoln, however, effortlessly kept pace. It swerved to tap his front fender, knocking Tubby off-kilter and onto a nonexistent shoulder. Tin cans and rocks banged against the Camaro's undercarriage. He was zooming straight at a row of mailboxes marking the turnoff to a side road.

A loud crack and a flash in the night. "They're shooting my tires!" he thought. Right before crashing into the mailboxes he yanked the wheel hard to the right. He took out at least one of the posts, doing untold damage to his car's bodywork, and gyrated madly down the side dirt road with all four tires still in commission.

Tubby simultaneously cut his headlights and gave it lots of gas. Sightlessly he went flying into a web of farms and fields with no illumination other than the moon and the dots of burglar floodlights standing watch over distant garages and tractor sheds. Thick woods crowded in from both sides. There were no people here.

He stuck to the middle of the rutted roadway, hearing stones ricochet off his pan, seeing and then not seeing the headlamps of the pursuing vehicle. He picked the left fork at a crossroads, then took another left into a grassy path marked "No Trespassing. Occidental Tree Farm." He quickly bashed into a dense stand of scraggly pine plantings, where the car came to a rest. Tubby turned the engine off.

The pursuing vehicle was out there somewhere. Tubby could almost hear it. Far away a semi downshifted and gunned its engine on the highway. In time, these human sounds faded away. Insects and cicadas buzzed.

Tubby gave his car a good long rest. The night's noises, crickets and tree frogs, and what might have been a barn owl, got louder. Way off, he thought he heard a woman's voice calling—maybe telling someone it was time to come inside for bed. He got his breathing under control and swatted a bug.

After another fifteen minutes he turned the key and was a little surprised that the Camaro started up. It was almost buried in the shrubbery. Backing out without lights, he no longer cared about scratches on his paint. Worse things could and probably would happen. Very slowly he tried to retrace his steps, but was soon lost on the dirt roads. At least he was alone. Finally, aided by luck, he reached Highway 25 and had a decision to make. He did not believe that his assailant was an insane stranger who just liked shooting at people. He believed him to be a calculating murderer from New Orleans who intentionally wanted to kill him. If so, danger was to the city in the south, and refuge was to the horse farm in the north, back toward the protective arms of Peggy O'Flarity.

Tubby made his turn and went a mile in the dark before an oncoming truck beeped at him until he flipped on his headlamps. Driving slowly, checking all his mirrors, he found himself again at the O'Flarity driveway. Carefully and cautiously, he turned in. The house was dark when he parked out front, but a security lamp automatically switched on when he got out of the car.

There was a rustling noise inside when he rang the bell. A curtain by the door parted, then the door opened. She was wearing a plush white robe, and her hair was mussed up.

"Uh," he said and held out his hands.

"You want a cup of coffee?" she asked. "You look like you've seen the *loup-garou.*"

XXII

A lot happened while Tubby was away. On that same Saturday morning while he was lingering over eggs at the diner, Cherrylynn found out that her boyfriend, Rusty, had not come home during the night. She knew he wasn't in her bed, obviously, but neither was he on the sofa, where he sometimes crashed if he came in plastered. She thought about calling him up and speaking her mind then and there, but it dawned on her that she just didn't care. This had been going on for too long, ever since he quit his offshore job. To say it straight, she was over him. This was a liberating revelation.

Delivering the news to Rusty wasn't going to be much fun though. He had never dared to get violent with her, but he sure could get loud. Cherrylynn pondered this over a cup of herbal tea and made up her mind. She stuffed all of her boyfriend's clothes and junk into the suitcase and duffle bag he stowed in a closet, then put them outside onto the apartment's tiny front porch. She set the deadbolt on the front door so that it could only be opened from within.

Suddenly she was in a hurry to get out of there and avoid a confrontation, with all the yelling and door-pounding that might entail. She ran to grab her purse, a banana, and a yogurt and exited out the back. She had never given Rusty a key to that door.

Cherrylynn jumped into her Civic and, under a canopy of pink crape myrtles, she bumped out onto the street. Where could she go to kill a few hours? One of her girlfriends was in Atlanta for the weekend, and the other one wouldn't be up this early on a Saturday. Might as well go to the office where there was Wi-Fi and parking. On the way she could drop off Tubby's decibel register at Raisin's girlfriend's house.

* * *

Also on Saturday, before lunch, Jason Boaz went to Confession. His church had a new priest. He was a young guy whom Jason hoped he could relate to on a contemporary and worldly basis.

The penitent had to bide his time in the pews until a blue-haired woman finally emerged from the confessional, looking chastened and tired. There is nothing that woman could possibly need to confess, he thought to himself, but perhaps he was wrong. As soon as the light turned green, he hurried up the aisle and into the box.

Through the grill, he could make out the faint features of the priest.

"In the name of the Father, and of the Son, and of the Holy Spirit, my last confession was two years ago," he began.

"All right, my son, have you denied your faith?"

"Not at all, Father." He would never do that.

"Have you profaned the use of God's name in your speech?"

"Not very often, Father."

"How about honoring Sundays?"

"Guilty, Father."

"Sexual thoughts about someone to whom you are not married?"

"Yes, Father. I know that's wrong. I mean, I guess. Whatever. But what I want to confess to is that think I may be killing somebody."

"That's very serious. In what sense do you mean that?"

"In the literal sense, Father. You see, I've built a miniature explosive device, which I've given to a man, and it's set to go off and kill him under certain circumstances."

"What circumstances?"

"Loud music. Actually, any very loud noise. You see…" and here Jason prattled on for a few minutes about how the device worked.

The priest let him talk until he wound down.

"Why did you do this?" the clergyman finally asked.

"It's a long story," Jason said, wanting to rush through this part, "but I was told to do it by some people that, frankly, I'm very afraid of."

"Do you mean to say that you fear for your life?"

"Yes, I do," Jason said earnestly.

"Well, you'll just have to trust that the Lord will protect you. But you know that you absolutely have to stop this thing from blowing up."

"I suppose you're right." He knew this would be the answer.

"Good, because if you don't intend to call it off, I may have to tell the police about this Confession."

Jason was astounded. "I thought this was private!" he exclaimed.

"There's an exception to everything," the young priest said.

"That certainly settles it then. I'll get in touch with the man as soon as I walk out of the church and tell him to drown that phone in the sink."

"You will have to take the consequences of this act as your penance. What else do you wish to confess?"

"I guess that's about it," Jason said.

"All right. Do your penance and you will be absolved. Go forth and sin no more."

"For His word endures forever," Jason mumbled as he hastened away.

But he couldn't reach Tubby on the phone. The lawyer was at that moment out of cell phone range, riding a horse over the hills of St. Tammany Parish.

* * *

Cherrylynn leafed through the small file she had created on Mr. Dubonnet's strange interest in the old shooting. She knew that her boss's conversation with the policeman whose father had originally investigated the matter, Detective Kronke, had failed to produce anything useful. But maybe she could use her feminine smarts to make something happen.

There was that handwritten name on a piece of paper found in the old police records—Bert Haggarty—and there was the scribbled impression of the name Carlos Pancera. She knew that Flowers, Tubby's private detective, was already making inquiries about Pancera. The possibility that she might cross paths with this investigator was very enticing, yet Tubby might not like her to be interfering. But what about this Haggarty? The note said "Indiana" beside his name, so she started there.

It was amazing how many oddball possibilities Google offered for that name. Scores, maybe hundreds. She thought about going into Westlaw but, at fifty-nine dollars per individual profile, Mr. Dubonnet would have a cow. She searched for the big cities in Indiana, since personally she couldn't name any, and then ran through the White Pages available for Indianapolis, Bloomington, Evansville, etc. That gave her nearly two hundred more Haggarties, but only one Bert, and he was in Fort Wayne. Of course Bert may have been the name of the victim, or the victim's now-deceased parent, or Bert might live in the country and not be in the city directories, or he might not have a phone, or… the chances were poor that this one name could be her guy. And what was she supposed to say when she called him? "Sir, do you know anything about a boy that got shot in New Orleans forty years ago?"

Why not? All it took was nosiness and nerve, and she had both. She called the number. A man's voice said, "Hello?"

"My name is Cherrylynn Resilio. I work for a lawyer in New Orleans. Do you possibly have any connection with a shooting that occurred in this city in or about the 1970s?"

"What did you say?"

She repeated her question.

"Of course not. What are you selling?"

"I'm not selling anything."

"Well, quit bothering people. I'm in the middle of changing diapers."

"So sorry…" was all she got out before the line went dead.

I guess I could do that two hundred more times, she thought, but that would be no fun. What if Bert Haggarty had moved to Minnesota or Montana, which in Cherrylynn's recollection were the states next to Indiana. The exercise was pointless.

Back to Carlos Pancera? She consulted Google again and had much better luck. He had been on the Board of the Latin American Cultural Society and had attended a gala given by Caribbean Freedom touted as a "Cuba Libre and Lime Night," music by Bodega Brass, tickets $250. He was an elder of the St. Agapius Catholic Church. He had received an honorary degree from Loyola University in recognition of his contributions to cultural understanding, presented by the Dean of the College of Social Sciences.

Now that was an interesting lead. Cherrylynn was taking a course on "The Politics of Rock and Roll" in that very department and her teacher, a young assistant professor named Mister Prima, possibly had a crush on her. They addressed him as "Mister," but his first name was Oliver. He gave all the students his home number.

"Oh, hi, Cherrylynn." Her name must have popped up on his phone since she had called him once before about a reading assignment.

He said he didn't mind talking to her on a Saturday, and, yes, he knew who Pancera was. There was a lot to the man's story, more than could be covered on the phone, and anyway Oliver was busy at the moment.

But, as it turned out, he would be free later. He was in fact in his office all day, catching up on some research. He could see her in the evening, on campus. She was so satisfied with this outcome that she hummed a tune to herself while checking her hair in a pocket mirror.

She was on a roll. She figured that Officer Sandoval would not be working today, since the Police Records office was undoubtedly closed, but she did have his cell number.

"Yeah?" His voice was as brusque as she remembered it. Just like a cop should sound.

"Hi, Officer. This is Tubby Dubonnet's assistant, Cherry-lynn?"

"Yeah?" he said again, but his voice seemed to soften a little.

"I did appreciate your finding that old file for us, but there really wasn't much in it."

"You got all there was."

"I don't suppose there is anyplace else you could look?"

"Not a chance. I don't know much about how records were kept back then. I was just a young man myself."

"One of the names in the report was Carlos Pancera. Is it possible that there would be some material about him?"

"I don't know the man."

"Oh, I wasn't suggesting that you did. I just wondered if you might look."

"You think I'm a librarian for a living? I'm a cop, and right now I'm frying catfish for a bunch of people."

"I know you're a policeman, and I know you are stuck in a job below your skills, but if there is any way you can help me I'd be really grateful."

"Maybe," he said grudgingly. "I'll look on Monday."

"Thank you so much. Shall I spell the name?"

"No. I got it. Bye." He hung up.

XXIII

Professor Prima's office was on the second floor of the Academic Building, and it wasn't big. He was sitting behind a very neat desk reading a small red book, which for no reason Cherrylynn thought might be poetry, while listening to soft Baroque music on the radio. His little window looked out upon a towering palm tree.

"Ah, Miss Resilio," he began. The professor was thin and metro in all ways. He was meticulously clean-shaven, and his black hair was neatly combed above his ears. He had on a loose-fitting blue Northface V-neck sweater, which revealed the hint of a silver necklace on his chest.

"Hi, Oliver," she said, sitting down. "Thanks for taking time to see me."

"I keep office hours almost every day, though I think you are the first student I've ever seen on a Saturday. Did you say you were interested in Señor Pancera?"

"Yes. I saw that he got an honorary degree here last year, and I thought maybe you could tell me something about him."

"Why the interest?" The professor closed his red book and swiveled around in his chair to put it in the bookcase built below the window. Cherrylynn thought he had surprisingly broad shoulders for a thin man and a college teacher at that. Maybe he had a personal trainer.

"His name came up in a case my boss, Tubby Dubonnet, is working on. He's a lawyer downtown."

"Don't guess I know him." Mister Prima spun back around. He gave her a bright smile. "Does the case have anything to do with Cuba?"

"Not that I know of. I think it is a homicide that happened a long time ago. Carlos Pancera probably had nothing to do with it. His name was just written on the inside of a file."

"Really." The professor inspected his fingers. "Pancera is a prominent Cuban refugee who has been very generous to the Catholic church and to this university. In fact, he is a big contributor to our department."

"How does he make his living?"

"I think he owns real estate."

"So, nothing shady in his background?"

"Nothing has ever been proven though years ago there were lots of myths and rumors about him—about our entire refugee community in fact."

"What sort of rumors?" Cherrylynn loved rumors.

"They've all been debunked, but do you know who Lee Harvey Oswald was?"

"Of course. The man who assassinated President Kennedy."

"Exactly. Did you know he lived in New Orleans?"

"I may have heard that, but I don't really remember. I wasn't born then."

"Naturally not. I wasn't either, but it is an important part of American history."

Chagrined, Cherrylynn lowered her eyes.

"While he was here in New Orleans," Prima continued, "he was active in what was called 'The Fair Play for Cuba Committee.' Some people speculated that, if indeed Oswald killed the president, his motive may have been his outrage over the Bay of Pigs fiasco. Kennedy launched the CIA-sponsored invasion force, which angered the pro-Castro people. Then Kennedy failed to support the attack, which lost us the best chance to overthrow Castro. Of course, Oswald may have had other motives. He spent two years in the Soviet Union and was married a Russian woman, so his true thinking is quite murky."

"What does that have to do with Mister Pancera?"

"Probably nothing, except that if Oswald had any supporters or financial backers, one might speculate that those sponsors could possibly have been found in a community passionate about Cuba, including the anti-Castro community."

"Wow."

"Yes, but that theory, in fact all theories, were rejected by the Warren Commission."

Cherrylynn did not know what the Warren Commission was, but that didn't matter. "So, it's not true?" she asked.

Mister Prima shrugged. "A lot of those Bay of Pigs fighters came from New Orleans, and a number of businessmen in this city paid good money to flight-train the Bay of Pigs pilots in Central America. They even provided an airfield in Nicaragua. I'm just saying there were a lot of serious hombres with military experience and violent attitudes in our fair city in those days. Their anger at being abandoned by the federal government got blended together with their hatred of the Civil Rights movement, which many of our local New Orleans community leaders believed to be Communist-led. There was fury and bloodlust aplenty in that period, and it wasn't even below the surface. It was the philosophy of the people who counted."

"I had no idea." To Cherrylynn, New Orleans had always been totally about fun.

"Oh yes," the professor continued. "I've written a paper about it."

"And Carlos Pancera was involved in all of that?"

"He was young then, but he came from a big family. He did

write some incendiary articles for the Latin newspapers. Yet I'd say he has never been much of a public figure. He asserted his influence mostly behind the scenes."

"Why did he get an honorary degree?"

"Pancera has been a great friend to our institution, and what I have just told you is all ancient history."

"Did these radical groups have names?"

"Yes, there was the Free Cuba Committee, as I said. There was also the Junior Anti-Communist League, though that sounds better in Spanish. There were the Defenders of Free Enterprise, and the Anti-Socialist Alliance. Quite a few groups actually, though I'd say their membership probably overlapped considerably."

He was almost drowned out by sirens blaring outside on St. Charles Avenue. It took a minute before they wound down. Cherrylynn used the time to scribble down the names the professor had just given her.

"Have there been books written about any of them?" she asked.

"Not really. There is my paper, of course, but it hasn't been published. You'd have to do original research. I had sort of a head start. My late father was actually in such a group. He told me a little bit about it. I've sometimes even imagined that I was under surveillance due to my interest in this subject."

His phone rang.

"Excuse me one second, Cherrylynn."

The teacher held his phone to his ear. His brow furrowed. He nodded without saying anything, then pocketed the phone and stood up.

"I'm very sorry, Miss Resilio, but I have another appointment now and we'll have to break this off."

"Sure," Cherrylynn said, backing out the door. "Can we talk again another day?"

"I've covered most of it," he said. "See you in class."

Calhoun Street, where she was parked, was blocked by fire trucks. Their rotating lights gave the neighborhood a carnival atmosphere. She tried to walk past them on the oak-lined sidewalk, but was stopped by a helmeted fireman.

"You can't get through this way, ma'am," he said. He had a big red mustache. "Go over and use the campus." He pointed off to his right.

"But my car is parked here."

"Yeah, what kind is it?"

"It's a blue Civic."

"Could be your car was just fire-bombed. Wait here a sec while I get a cop."

Her mouth fell open. Then she dug her phone out of her purse and tried to reach her boss. But Tubby was still out of range, driving in the country with his date for a nice dinner in Covington.

* * *

On that same Saturday evening, Raisin got to the Monkey Business Bar at about five o'clock after a strenuous day of playing tennis with his girlfriend, Sadie. She was tired and had no interest in going out for beer and music. She did ask if he wanted to join her at a party with people from her work at the oil company. They were all going to watch LSU battle Alabama on television. She promised there would be great food. Tickets on the fifty-yard line at Tiger Stadium might have gotten Raisin's attention, but otherwise he was not an LSU fan. And for some reason he wasn't that interested in eating any more.

But he did like to drink. So he did. By the time nine o'clock rolled around, after he had met everybody at the bar who was worth meeting, and just before the music was about to begin, he gave up his stool and took a fresh-air break outside.

The street was full of traffic, going places on a Saturday night. Raisin leaned against Janie's cypress siding and lit a cigarette. Screw quitting! He could smoke on his night off if he wanted to.

He watched a squirrel, nope, a big rat, traverse the power line overhead on an errand of its own. Inside the next band was tuning up. The chalkboard by the front door said this would be a group called "Roll of the Dice." A white Dodge Charger with a pretty female driver and a backseat full of girls stopped right in front of him. Because the driver and the passengers were all intent on their phones, he felt entitled to study them at length. But just when he was getting interested, they drove away.

"Wham!" the band started and the night came alive. Groups of people materialized from wherever they were huddled in their cars and crowded into the bar. By the time Raisin had stubbed out his first cigarette, a line was beginning to form outside. There was a twelve-dollar cover and maybe that would be an issue when he went back inside.

He stepped over the curb between two parked cars and pulled out the Samsung tester Jason Boaz had made. He fiddled around with it. He couldn't quite see what he was doing. Truth to tell, he was a little bit lit. After a couple of tries he sufficiently mastered the tiny keys to turn on a running video of whatever he pointed the camera at. A little more manipulation, following the distraction of a pack of women arriving in tight skirts, and he had a decibel reading. Ninety-eight points. Was that too high or too low? He didn't know, but he hit "Save."

The band was getting noisier, but something even louder began to intrude upon St. Claude Avenue's urban environment. Raisin looked down the street and beheld what looked to be a giant Mardi Gras float. Multi-colored lights flashed brightly and loud music blared from some serious amplifiers. It was shades of Monster Mudbug, the tow truck driver who wowed the city in crustacean costume and was Tubby's frequent client. Raisin could see, as the float came closer, a ring of women and men dancing ecstatically around it, waving feather boas and swirling hula hoops. But it wasn't Monster Mudbug. Not a crawfish in sight. The dancers all appeared to be naked, though the women were decorated with sparkle and sequins. Up top was a regal figure, playing the role of the King, though essentially a naked king. His throne was constructed from a maze of galvanized pipe. His Highness's scepter resembled an inverted Texas oil well. Behind him was a flashing LED screen that interspersed the name "Dinky Bacon" with black-and-white photographs from New Orleans' musical and architectural past. There was a confetti machine blasting bits of green paper, like shredded money, behind him. Pulling the spectacular contraption was a four-wheel-drive pick-up truck. A man crouched in the bed, filming the whole scene.

"Art is Free!" bellowed the speakers, drowning out the generator.

Raisin dug this action and flipped out his sound meter. He pointed it at the float, which was lighting up the sky for a block in all directions. The decibel level went steadily up and up, but Raisin's attention was grabbed by the hula-dancing girls. He jumped into the street to join them, but there were crowd-control chaperones alongside the float who objected.

"No photos! No video, old man!" A twenty-something biker-type wearing a leather vest slapped at Raisin's camera and sent the decibel-reader flying into the empty lot beside Ashton Monk's shotgun.

"Hey, dickhead!" Raisin who was incensed, grabbed for his assailant's leather collar and got his beard instead.

The disagreement was quickly forgotten when a deafening

161

explosion shook the street and rocked the walls of the bar. Raisin instinctively dived to the asphalt.

Porch lights came on up and down the block.

Raisin snuck a glance under his elbow to see the bearded giant crouching beside him, looking fearfully toward the heavens.

Raisin socked the guy where it hurt and made a run for his Miata. He locked himself inside, as the people emptied from the bar, running in all directions.

When the dust finally settled, it turned out that nobody who counted was hurt. Dinky Bacon's video went viral.

Raisin tried to reach Tubby to file a complaint, but his friend was cloistered inside a house in Folsom. Tubby had turned off his cell phone for fear that it might be used to track him by the night prowlers who had just tried to kill him.

XXIV

On Sunday morning, Tubby woke up in bed with a woman in a cotton nightgown, her back turned toward him. It took a moment to collect his thoughts. There had been an attempt on his life. He was sure about that. He had taken flight to this refuge. Warm arms had welcomed him.

His sleeping companion stirred. Tubby yawned and wished never to leave this room or this bed.

In time he and his hostess both did. They sat at the kitchen table drinking orange juice. He rehashed for her the story of the night before.

"I don't want to involve you," he assured her.

"That's good," Peggy said. "I do like living."

But, of course, he had involved her.

They discussed his options, but there was no way Tubby was going to spend the rest of his life hiding out here in the Florida Parishes. It was time to get on the road back home. The trouble would follow him there.

"At least you might consider taking another route back to the city," she suggested.

"If they want to try again in daylight they already know where you live and where I am. No, I'll just drive straight on in. I'm more worried about you."

"I have a groomsman to protect me and a carload of children coming over in an hour to ride horses. I'll take my chances."

Tubby pulled her close to him and kissed her. She pushed him away and patted his chest.

"That was nice," she said.

"This is probably a bad time for us to get serious about each other," he said.

"Like I said, I'll take my chances." She leaned into him, and he found his hand inside her nightgown cupping her breast.

His other hand slowly lifted the back of the gown and lightly caressed her bottom. She kissed him back and he was pressed against the kitchen counter. Tubby had planned to get on the road, but other needs were more immediate. He twirled them around. Now it was she who was against the counter, leaning backwards, and his hands couldn't stop.

* * *

Tubby pulled onto the blacktop, which was empty of traffic, and turned his Camaro south.

When he was almost to the Causeway, he violated a small law and turned on his cell phone. That was when he learned that he had missed quite a number of messages. Since he was maneuvering through Sunday morning church traffic, he didn't bother listening to them all, but he did press in a call to Cherrylynn.

"Boss, I've been trying to reach you!" she shouted.

"It's Sunday. What for?"

"I tried to call you yesterday! Somebody blew up my car! It's just, like, gone!"

"Oh, no! What happened?"

She told him in detail, which took long enough that he was

through the toll plaza and onto the bridge before she got to the end.

"And wait till you hear what happened to Mister Raisin!" And she was off again.

He didn't bother her with his own near-miss. At about Mile Marker 15, where he could see sailboats drifting afar and could imagine sunbathers arrayed on colorful towels on deck, he broke in and gave instructions.

He wanted to see her, Flowers, and Raisin if possible at his house at two o'clock sharp.

"You can take a cab," he told her. "I'll cover it."

* * *

In his living room an hour later, with the Saints versus the Seahawks game muted on the television, Tubby's team assembled. One by one they recounted their stories.

Cherrylynn's was the most interesting. They all were captivated by her description of the meeting with Professor Prima and her call to Officer Sandoval. Her car was totaled, and the police said it had to be arson. She had not been able to provide them with any possible explanation.

There had been a brief clip of the burned wreckage on Channel 4, but no suspects were named.

Flowers added that Trey Caponata had spent Saturday at the LSU football game and had tailgated with the Baton Rouge district attorney until almost midnight. The detective had also done some further digging on Carlos Pancera, though he acknowledged that Cherrylynn might have made more progress than he had. Tubby nodded, and she blushed at the compliment.

Flowers' tail on Pancera had revealed that the suspect had left his Broadmoor home at nine o'clock in the morning, had gone to mass at St. Agapius, and had not emerged until after one. Apparently he had an office somewhere in the church because his name was on a directory in the stair hall, but there was no room number. Upon leaving the church he went home, where he was at this moment. Also, he was a member of Kiwanis and was not registered to vote. Also, he had contributed between $500 and $1,500 to virtually every politician in the state.

"And we're talking St. Evangeline Parish Justice of the Peace," Flowers said by way of illustration.

Raisin's story was graphic and short. This was it:

"Boom! Your man's telephone was a bomb. It should have wasted me, but I am blessed."

Tubby told them what had happened to him. All in all, a sobering meeting.

"Here's what I want," he told the crew. "All of this has got to be related to me sticking my nose into that shooting back in the 1970's. Flowers, I want you to get inside that church, and Pancera's home if you can, and see if you can find any incriminating papers, pictures, anything."

"You figure Pancera is behind this?"

"I don't know. He's connected to men with violent histories. And the Babineaux shooting, too, and that detective, what's his name?"

"Victor Argueta."

"Yeah, him. And Archie Alonzo, the prima donna who sent our guy into harm's way, does he have any violent history? I wish we could get into the books of their police detail company."

Flowers was busily typing away on his iPad.

"Trey Caponata, the mafia wannabe…" Tubby continued, "what about him?"

"Do you see any angle?" Flowers asked.

"Probably not, but does he know anybody who can make a bomb?"

"Other than Jason Boaz?" Raisin threw in.

"Right. Somebody who can make a car bomb."

"Boaz has the skill," Flowers said.

"I guess," Tubby conceded, "but doesn't it sound like something a Mafioso would do?"

"Why would Caponata want to intimidate Cherrylynn and you?" Flowers asked.

"I don't know." Tubby was exasperated. "Someone has come close to killing my oldest friend Raisin." Raisin stood and took a bow. "And the very best secretary I have ever had. And me! All in one weekend. We have to find out who and why."

"I'll need to put a couple more people on this," Flowers said.

"Of course." The lawyer frowned. "Now, Cherrylynn, go rent a car and use my credit card. Follow up with all of that wonderful research and see if you can get us any more names of people who were involved in any of these Cuba groups. God knows why they would care about a dozen peaceniks demonstrating on Canal Street, but maybe. Keep on pumping Sandoval even if he's not likely to have anything new for us."

"What about me?" Raisin asked.

"Just take a break," Tubby told him. "And I'm going to have a talk with my old friend Jason Boaz."

"I'd like to spend some time with him myself," Raisin said.

"Me first." Tubby got up and the meeting was adjourned.

* * *

After everybody left, the first thing the lawyer did was walk around and, even though it was still daylight, turn on every light in the house. Then he went upstairs to locate and load his old

Colt .45. After that he drove to Jason Boaz's condo out by the lake. Because he lived in a big building and parked in its garage, you couldn't tell if Boaz was home until you knocked on the door.

Which Tubby did.

He heard a chair scraping the floor inside, but no one answered the knock.

"Open up, Jason!" Tubby yelled and pounded louder.

"Is that you?" a voice inside asked.

"Of course, it's me. Let me in."

The door swung open displaying Jason in a bathrobe. He looked like he hadn't shaved in a couple of days.

Tubby pushed past him and went into the living room with all of its orange and lime aluminum furniture. Tubby was packing a pistol this time, stuck in his belt by the small of his back and concealed by his jacket.

"Jeez, Tubby! This is a relief. I thought you might be dead."

"You tried hard enough to kill me, and you almost took out Raisin and a whole crowd of people parading in the street."

"No, I don't think the phone had sufficient range to take out a crowd. Three feet circumference, max."

"What are you talking about?" Tubby got in his face. "You've attempted murder."

Boaz cracked a little and collapsed back into a purple chair, almost tipping over backwards. "I tried to stop it, Tubby. I called you but you didn't answer. I tried to disconnect it remotely, but I just wasn't smart enough to figure out how to do it. I admit my offense. And here you are. My friend. I am so happy. How can you forgive me?"

"I can't forgive you, you crazy nutcase. We've known each other for years. I'm turning you over to the police. Really, you ought to be locked up in a padded cell."

"Tubby, please. Think of all the good times. All the winners I tipped you to at the Fairgrounds."

"Who were you afraid of enough to make you do this, this crazy thing?"

Boaz buried his head in his hands. "I can't tell you," he moaned. He recovered enough to pat his new beard.

"Last chance, Jason. I'm not fooling around, not with a maniac like you on the loose. Who was it? Pancera?"

At that name, Boaz hid his eyes behind the crook of an elbow and started to sob.

"This dude is stranger than a '610 Stomper,' " Tubby thought. Yet, strangely, his heart was starting to melt.

"This is all about something that happened when you were young, isn't it, Jason? Were you the one who shot the boy, the peace demonstrator? That day when all the traffic was stopped on Canal Street because Kissinger was in town. It's understandable. Back then there were only two worlds right? The Oakies from Muskogee and the hippies from San Francisco. You had to pick a side, right?"

"No," Jason whispered. His voice was almost inaudible. "None of that made sense to me. It was the 'Night Watchman.' "

Tubby wasn't sure he had heard right. "The Night Watchman?" he repeated.

"I didn't say that," Boaz whispered.

"Yes, you did. Who is that?"

"Forget that. It was just a title. We all had some dumb title. I was the 'Viper.' Short for vice-president. The Night Watchman, I made that up. He was in charge of the mission. Makes no sense, right?"

"So? What was his name?"

"That I can't say."

"Why not?"

"I took an oath, and they would kill me."

"That's ridiculous," Tubby said. "Was Pancera involved in all this?"

"He was the Recorder."

"What's that mean?"

"He kept the records. I don't know. I made it up."

"Who was the Leader?"

"I can't say his name."

"Nuts. What was the name of your group?"

"The 'Boys' Club.' I don't know. I can't say."

"Who was in it?"

"I can't say."

"You'd better say!" Tubby pulled the .45 out of his pants and pushed it into Boaz's forehead just below his bushy hairline.

"Go ahead and pull the trigger, Tubby. I deserve it. I've led a miserable life. I have sinned. Oh yes, I have…"

"Oh, shut up," Tubby cursed him. He holstered his automatic and yanked open the door to let in some fresh air. "Just look out for Raisin," he said in parting. Raisin had it in him to be mean, and sometimes he was cold enough to leave you holding a handful of your own teeth.

The 'Night Watchman,'" Boaz had said. So, the shooter hadn't been Pancera.

But Pancera knew who it was.

XXV

In the morning Tubby met Flowers for a cup of coffee at the Trolley Stop, a busy 24-hour joint on St. Charles Avenue where no one ever bothered you. Tubby had his coffee with half-and-half. Flowers had his coffee with the "Southern Special," consisting of three eggs over easy, hot biscuits and sausage gravy, four pieces of bacon, grits and butter, a slice of ham, and God knows what else.

"Very hungry," he said. "I was up all night."

He had gotten inside Pancera's house when the old man went out to nighttime mass. Then after Pancera went home, Flowers got inside the church.

"This was not exactly legal." He mentioned the obvious. "But I wasn't observed."

At the house Flowers had encountered, unfortunately, a housekeeper puttering about in the kitchen. Nevertheless, without being noticed, the detective was able to snoop around in Pancera's den, or office. The room held a worn brown leather couch piled high with papers, a matching leather chair pulled up to a desk also covered with same, lots of books and no computer. Undoubtedly Pancera had a safe somewhere, but Flowers didn't have time to look for it. Aside from bank statements and bills, there was unopened junk mail from dozens of political non-profits with names like the American Society for Tradition,

Family and Property and the Catholic League for Religious and Civil Rights; in short, nothing very enlightening.

There were two intriguing items, however. At the very bottom of one of the ceiling-high bookcases was a box of yellowing newspapers from Father Charles Coughlin's Little Flower Church in Detroit.

"I don't know what that is," Flowers admitted, "but the Father obviously hated Roosevelt and the Communists."

"Pancera must be a collector," Tubby said. "Those are from the 1930s. Coughlin was competing with Huey Long for the protest vote."

"Okay, so then it's way too dated to matter, but I thought maybe it was relevant."

"What else?"

"A plaque on the wall from 'The Marti Patriotic League' with the inscription, 'For Faithful Service', and below that the initials 'ACNI.'"

"So?"

"It had a date on it of June, 1977. I just thought, since it was from your time period, that I would mention it."

"I see. That's good. What about the church?"

"*De nada.* Pancera does have an office there, but it hasn't got a thing in it except bulletins and old orange peels. There is a safe on the floor and I popped it. Inside was a pile of little bills, maybe a thousand dollars, and a jelly jar full of loose change."

"Lots of dead ends."

Flowers was mildly crestfallen.

"Crossing possibilities off the list is important, too," he said. "At least that's what they teach us in detective school."

"I didn't mean to suggest it wasn't," Tubby said contritely. "That 'patriotic league' thing may be worth something. Let's call Cherrylynn."

Flowers didn't appear to be entirely pleased with this course of action, but Tubby dialed her up anyway. She was at the office, of course, and he gave her the name.

"Add it to your list," he said.

* * *

Cherrylynn was fully engrossed in her list. She was coming up with a lot of information about Cuban-American youth groups in the 1960s and 70s, but most of them were centered around Miami. There was not much on the web about the Cubans of New Orleans, except for a brief mention in a footnote to a Wikipedia article and some references to the Special Collections material at Tulane University. Maybe it would be worth a trip uptown to see what the Tulane campus library had to offer. That, however, would probably require coordinating with Mr. Dubonnet and his alumni ID card to get access.

But this last name, ACNI, struck a small but rich vein. It stood for Association for Cuban Nationalist Infantry, and there was an extensive write-up about it in something called the "CIA Counter-Revolutionary Handbook, Second Edition, 1985." She couldn't find any explanation of what this so-called CIA document actually was or how it had found its way onto the Internet, but sure enough, it identified the founders of ACNI as one Hector Boaz (b. 1932) and Pablo Pancera (b. 1930) in Santiago, Cuba. Were these the fathers of two currently suspicious characters? She'd bet her paycheck that Tubby would think so.

A major find! It told her that she was looking at the right group. But, of course, it didn't actually prove anything. The cryptic "CIA Handbook" entry described the mission of ACNI as "raising funds for anti-Castro military endeavors." That was about it. The CIA helpfully provided the Spanish spelling of the group's name, which was *La Asociación para la Infantería Nacionalista Cubano*. As an afterthought, Cherrylynn Googled that.

And here she found a link to a 1977 article in the New Orleans *Times-Picayune* headlined "Benefit Honors Rich Heritage." Click.

It had appeared on the newspaper's Society Page, where New Orleans' daily gatherings of the glamorous and significant were described and where photographs of attendees, often clutching glasses of white wine, were displayed. The ACNI party at the Marriott Hotel Grand Ballroom had been one of the events highlighted in the Sunday edition of the paper, and it was described as a "Cultural Celebration of our Caribbean Character." The honoree was ACNI founder Pablo Pancera, who received the *Premio a la Libertad*. Other participants' names were also listed in bold. What jumped off the page at her was a picture of Pablo's son, Carlos Pancera, standing beside his wife, Maria. Scrolling over to the photographs of the event she found a picture of the elder Pancera standing between his son and his daughter-in-law. The men all wore tuxedos, the woman was in a blue gown. They all had very un-partylike expressions, and there were no wine glasses to be seen.

Below this somber family scene, another photo caught Cherrylynn's attention. Once again, an older man was featured with a younger man by his side. The older man was vaguely familiar, and when she enlarged the page she saw his name, Patron Sandoval. To his right was his son, Ricardo Sandoval. Gee whiz! The Rick Sandoval she knew today looked just like his old man did in 1977.

Suddenly Tubby barged through the office doors trailed by a bearded stranger whose black shirt was unbuttoned to display his hairless sculpted chest. Another man in jeans, wearing a cowboy hat and carrying a camera on his shoulder, was in hot pursuit.

"Boss, I've got something big!" Cherrylynn shouted.

"Cherrylynn, this is Dinky Bacon. I know you've heard a lot

about him. The great visual and physical display artist? We're going to be here for just a few minutes."

"But this is something…" The secretary paused when the camera swung toward her and resumed with, "Come right on in. We have a really important case breaking right now, but we are also deeply committed to the arts of New Orleans." She gave the camera her big smile.

Tubby beamed at her and waved his guests ahead and into his office.

The cameraman immediately zoomed in on the view from the window, which pretty much encompassed everything in the Crescent City from the river to the Lake.

"I could do wonders with a space like this," Dinky Bacon glowed.

"We could use some more art in here, that's for sure," Tubby chimed in, "but fully dressed, you understand."

The camera caught the artist laughing.

"It's a grave injustice," Tubby said, apropos of nothing. The camera again swung his way. "This city has traditions of free expression going back hundreds of years, whether it's political rhetoric, fine literature, grand architectural monuments like the Superdome, or just plain eccentric behavior. Dinky Bacon deserves international recognition, not persecution, and we will see that he gets his day in court."

"Cut," the cameraman said.

"Thanks a bunch, Mister Dubonnet." His client pumped his hand.

"Don't forget your court date next Wednesday," Tubby reminded him.

"I'll be there," the cameraman and Dinky said in unison.

The lawyer showed them out.

* * *

"What was that, boss?" Cherrylynn asked.

"Pro bono," Tubby said innocently. "Whatcha got for me?"

"I've got you Police Officer Rick Sandoval," she said proudly, and showed Tubby what she had printed off the net.

XXVI

The plan had Cherrylynn calling Sandoval, following up on her new request for records. She would invite the policeman downtown to Tubby's office, using her charms, where he could be confronted by both Tubby and Flowers. The plan, however, went immediately awry.

"I found another file on this Pancera guy you asked about," Sandoval said. "But this is all irregular. I'm not handing it over to you. I've got to watch my ass. If your boss wants it, I'll give it to him."

"Oh, that's fine, Officer," Cherrylynn said. Tubby was listening in on his line and making thumbs up signs to his secretary. "You can bring it here to the office. I'll make a copy and hand the file back to you."

"No, thanks. Tell him I'll meet him the same place we talked last time."

"Let me see..."

Tubby broke in. "Meet you at the same place? You mean at Le Bon Temps?"

"Right. I'll be in the parking lot out back. I get off at four. You can be there at four-thirty."

Tubby agreed. Then he lined up Flowers. They would do this together.

"He doesn't know we suspect him of anything," Tubby

said, "so I wouldn't expect any trouble. We'll show him the newspaper picture Cherrylynn found and see if he opens up about the shooting of a peace demonstrator."

"I'm in, Tubby, but he's not going to say much" was Flowers' opinion. "You've got nothing on him, and he wears a badge."

* * *

Their plan went awry again. Flowers and Tubby, in separate cars pulled into the gravel parking lot across the street from the Bon Temps bar. The sun was still out, still hot, and the only other car in the lot was a police cruiser.

"I thought he'd be off-duty," Tubby said into his phone, which was communicating with Flowers. "I wasn't expecting the car."

"Hmmmm" was what he got in response.

They each got out, and Sandoval got out. Unlike at their last meeting at the bar, the policeman was fully uniformed and wearing his intimidating belt with its gun, radio, night stick, handcuffs, and Taser.

"Hey," Tubby said, extending his hand. Sandoval looked at it for a second before he shook it. The two men were almost eye-to-eye. Tubby was heavier across the middle. Sandoval was squared off like a solid block of wood.

"Who's this guy?" Sandoval asked.

"He's Sanré Fueres, a private detective. He worked some with Ireanous Babineaux."

"Hi," Flowers said. They didn't shake hands.

"I've got one file. It's in the back seat." The cop opened the rear door of his NOPD Crown Vic. "Get in and we can talk."

Flowers was shaking his head, but Tubby slid into the seat and reached for the manila folder.

Sandoval slammed the door.

"Beat it!" he told Flowers.

"No way! Let him out of there!"

Tubby had found that the folder contained blank sheets of paper. He was beating on the window.

Sandoval pulled out his badge and shoved it into Flowers' face.

"He's a suspect. Illegal possession of records. You are, too. Bend it over!" He pushed Flowers over the trunk of his police car. "I'm going to arrest you," he said. "Spread those legs." He had a hand on his Taser.

This wasn't Flowers' first rodeo. Tubby watched as Flowers complied, grim-faced, but without protest. Sandoval efficiently patted him down, then yanked the detective's arms back and slapped cuffs on his wrists.

"Now," the cop said. "We're going back to your car." Tubby was trying to kick out the glass.

"Keep it up and you're in the hospital," Sandoval yelled over his shoulder. He pushed Flowers into the back seat of the detective's big GMC Yukon.

"Your PI license is on the line, dude," Sandoval told him. "And there's a special place in the Mississippi River for private dicks who get in my way." He slammed the door.

Returning to his police car, Sandoval straightened his shirt and gave his backseat passenger a glare. He checked the vicinity to see if anyone was watching, which apparently they were not, then got in and started up.

"What the hell do you think you're doing?" Tubby demanded from behind him, imprisoned by the mesh shield. "I'm a lawyer!"

"I don't care what you are," Sandoval told him. "Shut up or I'll tase your pecker."

Tubby swallowed the several paragraphs about Constitutional rights he was about to deliver and shut up. Squirming around to look, he saw Flowers' parked car recede in the distance. Sandoval took a right on Magazine and headed toward Audubon Park.

They got to River Road, up near Cooter Brown's, and Sandoval slowed down. Right before Carrollton Avenue, he entered a cramped parking lot outside a small concrete block building badly in need of paint. There was a sign outside that read, "For Rent," with a suggestion after that: "Mardi Gras Floats?"

Sandoval pulled Tubby out of the cruiser at gunpoint, used a key to unlock the solid steel door, and pushed Tubby inside. It was dark, but the cop popped a switch, and the dingy space was brightened with fluorescent ceiling lights that hissed. There were no Mardi Gras floats there. Tubby's focus was on a single chair in the middle on the concrete floor.

"Have a seat," Sandoval said as he pulled the metal door shut with a clang.

Tubby rushed the cop and got a nightstick in the nose for his trouble. He staggered back and would have fallen on the concrete if he hadn't hit the chair first.

"Let's reach an understanding," Sandoval said, wiping his lips with his hand. "This is going to hurt you a lot worse than it hurts me."

Blood dripped from the lawyer's nose, but he held his head up.

"Ah. Ah," he sighed, trying to shake off the pain.

"You're in a bad place, counselor," Sandoval said. He produced a rope from somewhere in the confined room.

Approaching Tubby, he explained, "I'm going to tie you up. If you don't like it I'll bust a couple of your ribs first. Believe me, there are no cameras in here."

Tubby submitted, his head swirling too fast to think of an alternative. Quickly, his hands were bound together, then to the chair. Then his legs were tied together. He had never in his life felt so helpless, except maybe when one of his MP wrestling buddies had squashed his face into the mat.

Mission accomplished, Sandoval went to a corner and spoke into his phone.

"Relax," he said when he came back. "You've got a few minutes."

* * *

There had been an afternoon, back in Naples, when it was raining and the wind was blowing, making white caps in the bay and tossing the palms around like mop heads. Tubby, secure behind the glass doors to the balcony, thought that maybe he would like it here. The condo towers were obscured by low clouds, the Jaguars on the street had retired, and the sea, with its stirring elemental power, reminded him that this was a real place and not a mere movie set. It was seductive to watch the torrential rain washing over the porch and cascading down in tropical waterfalls from the balcony above.

Marguerite's larder in the coziness of her apartment was filled with expensive cheeses and wine. On the kitchen counter was a bag of fresh stone crabs just waiting to be cracked and eaten.

Now, tied to a folding chair in a barren concrete warehouse, he could not remember why he had thrown away the chance to live amidst such heavenly delights. In utopia. What could he have been thinking?

* * *

The door creaked open and admitted Carlos Pancera. Tubby knew him only from pictures, but the man had a fierce presence that was memorable and commanded respect. There were two others with him, both of them old-timers like Pancera. One was slender, with gray hair and a deeply lined face. He wore a clerical collar. The other was big, like Tubby, and red-faced with jowls that sagged over a large neck. He was wearing a black Saints sweatshirt over a major potbelly. He looked vaguely familiar. Tubby wondered whether Jason Boaz might be the next one through the door.

The three men huddled with Sandoval for a minute, conversing in low voices out of Tubby's hearing, though he picked up faint allusions to "asshole" and "troublemaker." Sandoval fetched more folding chairs from a stack by the wall and arranged them in a half-circle facing their captive. In the spare shadowy room, Tubby was reminded of a séance he had once witnessed while working on a case. Perhaps José Marti would be summoned from the great beyond. Or Fulgencio Batista. Or Parker.

"Who are you guys?" he asked. His mouth was dry. Blood was caking on his lips.

"You know who I am," Pancera said, his voice like a hammer. "You've been asking all over town about me. And who are you? Some unimportant person who can't mind his own business?"

"You want to know who shot that hippie forty years ago?" Sandoval demanded. "Well, I did."

"No, you didn't. It was me," the fat man said, and Tubby could have believed him. He had mean pig eyes. There was just a hint in that boozy face of the angry boy he might have been.

"Enough from both of you," Pancera ordered. "The point is that it was a patriotic act. It instilled fear in the enemy."

"He was just a kid," Tubby said, exploring the knots binding his wrists with his fingertips, seeking a flaw.

"None of us were kids," Pancera said scornfully. "We were

all young men with brothers and fathers dying around the world fighting socialism. What matter if you killed the enemy in Bolivia or Southeast Asia or New Orleans? It was war."

"Yeah? Who won?" Tubby baited him.

"We did," the fat man said.

"What about Cuba?" Tubby asked. "It's still the same as it was fifty years ago."

Pancera answered him. "That cause is still unfinished, but one day Cuba will be free. The men you see here now are not too old to fight, and we also have resources."

The priest, silent till now, added, "I will say Mass again in Havana. I can promise you that. In the very church where I took my first communion."

"What's your part in this, Sandoval?" Tubby asked the cop. "Why did you turn over the police file to me?"

"Shut up, turd!" Sandoval stole a quick glance at Pancera and the fat man, who also looked momentarily puzzled. "I'm the one who protects this group by rooting out infiltrators and eliminating little worms like you."

"Eliminate me!" Tubby blustered. "My detective saw you taking me away."

"You died trying to escape, and he will also, soon enough."

"If you're going to kill me, what's all this hocus-pocus about?"

"Who are you working for, Mister Dubonnet?" the priest asked gently, resuming the interrogation.

"I'm a lawyer," Tubby said. "I work for clients."

"You're a crud communist," the fat man said. "I can smell one in a crowd. Who do you really work for?"

"Nobody. I'm not working for anybody. To me this is only about seeing justice done. Don't you get it? This kid died in my arms."

"Ah, so you say you just happened to be walking down the street when a gun went off?"

"No, I was with the demonstrators, but…"

"You admit it!"

"We were all kids. I went into the Army."

"Do you work for the government?" Pancera wanted to know. "Hollywood? Are you writing a book? Is it the Kennedy assassination you are investigating?"

"I have no interest whatsoever in the Kennedy assassination. I think it happened when I was in third grade."

"You lie through your teeth," Sandoval grumbled.

"What's the connection? I just don't get it."

"I think he needs a couple of whacks," the fat man said.

Desperate to change the direction this interrogation was taking, Tubby broke in with, "Why did Officer Babineaux have to die?"

"He was like you and stuck his nose into places it didn't belong," Sandoval said.

"But he was your partner, your friend."

"You think that," Sandoval said angrily. "He tried to blackmail me into dumping our union president. Alonzo was cutting him out of the business and keeping me in. Babineaux didn't go for that and threatened me. Some friend, huh?"

"What could he threaten you with?"

Pancera held up his hand palm out to stop the talk. He addressed Tubby. "Let's just say that we have records going back many years. Our struggle will be chronicled one day in the history books. But the time to make those records public has not yet come. Unfortunately, that black policeman Babineaux you speak of had been given those records for safekeeping by Mister Sandoval after the levees broke during Katrina, since Officer Sandoval's house was severely flooded. Babineaux was high and dry uptown, and he was heavily fortified in his house.

Unfortunately for your policeman, he had too much time on his hands and read those records. He decided to use them for his own purpose, which was to threaten, I'll call it blackmail, Officer Sandoval for personal advantage. This had to do with some petty dispute he and Sandoval were having about controlling off-duty police assignments. None of that had or has a thing to do with the rest of our group or the historic movement we have been a small part of. Those records are invaluable and of vital interest to us and to history. It was very unwise of him to threaten us in that way."

"So you killed him?"

Tubby directed that at Pancera, but the policeman and the fat man both laughed.

"No," Pancera said drily. "I can't say that I killed anyone. But I was happy to see him gone. I was happy to see our records returned to us for our posterity."

"Perhaps," the priest broke in, "this man is not going to answer our questions."

"I can make him talk," Sandoval said.

The priest rose from his folding chair and straightened his back. "Life is full of mysteries," he said vaguely. "We may have to live with the mystery of this man and his motives, even after he has gone to his grave. But," he added, "if you want to try to pry it out of him, my strong friend, I won't stop you. I, however, am leaving."

"I'm staying," the fat man said.

"I will drive Father home," Pancera told the group. "You two can take care of everything here."

XXVII

When Flowers drove up to the warehouse, he saw Sandoval's police car parked in the small lot in front of the building and a Mercedes Benz pulling away, with a hood ornament to rival the Vince Lombardi Trophy. He considered following the car but decided to stick with the cop. He rolled slowly into the lot. As he parked, he saw a figure dash furtively from the shadows and disappear behind the police car.

Flowers got out and approached with caution. Jason Boaz stood up and showed himself. He raised his hands.

"What's going on?" Flowers asked, showing a gun.

"He's in there," Boaz whispered. "I have a key."

Flowers took it out of Boaz's hand and popped the door open as quietly as he could. The scene inside was two big men slapping Tubby around. Flowers pushed Jason out of the way and walked in with his gun waving wildly.

"Up! Up!" he yelled.

The bigger man did not appear to be armed. He stepped back from Tubby, who had his bloody chin on his chest. As he tried to raise it, Flowers saw Tubby's tongue moving around in his cheeks, counting teeth. Blood had collected on his shirt.

"This is police business, asshole!" Sandoval protested. "Stay out of it!"

"Bullshit," Flowers said calmly, taking two steps forward. "Boaz, do you have a camera?"

The inventor stepped into the room and his phone flashed.

"Both of you boys step back," Flowers ordered. "Officer Sandoval, remove your firearm from your belt and place it carefully on Mr. Dubonnet's lap."

Reluctantly they did what they were told. "Both of you, out the door," Flowers said, scooping the .40 caliber.

Sandoval affected a swagger as he walked past the detective, and the fat one audibly growled, but they moved toward the exit with Flowers a pace behind. The detective was sure that Sandoval had more weapons on his person and probably more in his police car.

"Get Tubby untied," he told Boaz over his shoulder. With care, he escorted the policeman and his hood friend to Sandoval's official vehicle.

Jason succeeded in cutting Tubby loose with the Leatherman Super Tool he always carried.

"Glad to see you," his former lawyer mumbled.

"I just couldn't let this happen," Jason told him. "Can you walk?"

"Babe, I can run," Tubby said. "Let's get out of here."

With a little help, the lawyer made it out the door and into the parking lot to see Flowers holding the cop and the fat man in front of the cruiser. "Get in my car, Tubby," Flowers instructed, and then addressed Sandoval. "I've got pictures. They're on the Cloud now. Whether they stay there all nice and quiet depends on you. I know you have a gun in your car. Or several. But what's done is done. Just drive away. Right?"

Sandoval sneered while the fat man got into the passenger seat. "I'll get back to you another day," he whispered to Flowers.

"*Tu mama es una piruja*," Flowers whispered back.

Red-faced, the policeman got behind the wheel and Flowers quickly stepped behind his own car to protect himself. He braced his elbows on the hood and leveled his pistol at the cop's shady face behind the windshield.

But there was no gunfire. The cop and the fat man peeled off onto River Road. Flowers, with Jason Boaz looking over his shoulder, watched the tail lights recede. But just a couple of blocks away, the car slowed and cut left across a curb. It stopped in the gravel beside the Public Belt Railroad tracks. He couldn't tell if anyone got in or out.

"That doesn't look good," Flowers said.

"Wait," Boaz said.

A flash of light enveloped the police car. A split second later a wave of hot air and the crash of the explosion hit them. Both men fell to the ground instinctively.

"What was that?" Flowers shouted, almost unable to hear himself.

"We should get out of here," Jason said.

The police car was a flaming wreck.

"Copy that!" Flowers yelled, lunging behind the wheel of his SUV, where Tubby was huddled in the passenger seat, bleary with one eye shut.

"Did you do that?" the detective cried out the window to Boaz.

"Yes, I did," Jason said. "I've learned how to control the device better now."

He waved goodbye to Flowers, or maybe to the youth movement he had been a part of so many years ago, and faded back into the darkness.

Flowers wasted no time aiming his vehicle back toward Audubon Park. Behind him he could see people running toward the burning car. Sirens were coming from everywhere.

"Jesus," Flowers said to Tubby. "Your friends."

"Strange bunch, aren't they?" Tubby gave a small laugh, which ended in a cough.

Police cars and an EMT van passed them going in the other direction. Tubby's own car was still in the bar's dark parking lot, where he had left it.

"Can you drive?" Flowers asked. "Do you want to go to the hospital or anything?"

"No, I think I can make it." He had been feeling his jaw, around his eyes and his rib cage. "I don't think they broke anything. In fact, I feel pretty good."

"Were others there?" Flowers asked. "I saw a big Mercedes leaving when I drove up."

"That was Carlos Pancera and some very bad priest," Tubby told him. "Call Jason tomorrow and make him give you the man's name. They didn't hang around for the dirty work."

"Who was that guy with Sandoval, the one who got blown up?"

"We were never introduced, but I heard him called 'Jefé'. I think he was the 'Leader.' "

"And Pancera?"

"I'm told he was the 'Recorder.' "

"And Sandoval?"

"Security."

"Who was the Night Watchman?"

"I'm not sure, but maybe the one who killed Babineaux, blew up Cherrylynn's car, and tried to get me. That vicious priest is a likely candidate."

"Okay, that's clear as mud. I'll follow you home."

"No need for that."

"I'll follow you, anyway."

"How did you find me?" Tubby asked.

"After I unlocked the cuffs, which I must say is a pretty extraordinary feat, I tracked his police car on my GPS. He's got a built-in buzzer, like all the cops, and I have the code. I could know where every police car in the city is, if I wanted to."

"Really? Well, good night."

With Flowers trailing behind, the lawyer drove home for some liquid painkiller.

XXVIII

The next morning Tubby arrived at his office late with a black eye. Cherrylynn made over him like an Ursulines nun until he demanded that she get back to her desk and find some work to do.

The news on the radio, web, and TV had a lot of misinformation about the explosion that had killed a police officer. Only one victim was mentioned. The head of the police union was demanding that locals be permitted to conduct the investigation without involving any federal "gestapo" from Alcohol, Tobacco and Firearms.

Flowers called to say that Boaz would not answer the phone, but he had another idea.

"I sent you an email," the detective said. "It's a copy of a page from the St. Agapius Church website with a picture of the last priest, who retired. His name is Escobar. If you can open it up, it might be your man."

Tubby powered up his laptop and took a look. A slightly younger and more trustworthy-looking image of his interrogator appeared. "That's him," he said. "Can you find out where he lives?"

"I already know that. It's on Belfast Street, up by St. Rita's."

"I'd like to get inside his house when he's not there."

"Easy enough. For what?"

"Old records. They said they had records going back decades. Ireanous Babineaux had them, and he got killed for them. What better place to keep them now than with the Night Watchman?"

"You think he's the one? I'll see if I can get inside today."

"I'm going with you."

"I don't think that's such a good idea. I get paid for taking risks like that."

"It was me who got my head pounded. You keep watch on the house. Tell me when it's clear. I'll be close, and my phone is in my pocket."

* * *

Father Escobar had a friend, a church sexton named Marcos, who picked the priest up most afternoons to go shopping and visit sick people. Flowers deduced that within six hours. On the following day he had Tubby meet him on Belfast at 1:30. Sure enough, the sexton appeared on schedule and parked his white Saturn in front of Father Escobar's house. Marcos got out, a tired-looking man in a rumpled brown suit, and approached the front door. He was admitted and a few minutes later reemerged with the priest behind him. They got into the Saturn and drove away toward Fontainebleau.

Observing this from a block away, Tubby and his sleuth exited the detective's Jimmy SUV and casually strolled along the sidewalk. They were surprised by a young jogger in sweats who passed them pushing her red baby stroller. She barely seemed to notice them. She had a phone to her ear.

Flowers turned into the priest's driveway, which served as the divider between their target and the neighbor's house. Tubby fell in step. At the rear of the house narrow concrete steps led up to a back entrance sheltered under a dirty aluminum awning. Flowers ascended in one long stride and, so swiftly that Tubby didn't even see it, he torqued open the back door and slipped inside. The lawyer hurried in after him.

They were in a small laundry room adjoining an old-fashioned kitchen, the kind common in New Orleans houses that haven't been renovated since the fifties. It had wooden kitchen cabinets painted in lime sherbet, a black and white tiled linoleum floor, a small rickety yellow table with the morning breakfast dishes still on it, and a white enameled sink, its discolored chrome fixtures dotted with corrosion. The room was lit by a pair of fluorescent tubes on the ceiling that buzzed and blinked faintly when Flowers clicked on the switch.

"Not a rich man," the detective whispered. He seemed relieved. If one dug deeply, which Tubby had, one would find that Flowers came from a culture that didn't believe that priests, even the bad ones, should ever be rich.

The next dim room was being used as an office. Past it, through tall French doors, was the parlor and beyond that the front door to the street. The office had intriguing filing cabinets, a desk and a large bookcase stuffed with magazines, and a stairway, marked by carved newel posts, led upwards.

Flowers ascended it. Tubby paused to size up the office and think about the man who worked here. There were a number of Bibles. The blinds were pulled down to shut out the sun. A ceiling fixture of slender plastic wands tipped with yellow candle-flame-shaped bulbs provided less light than what little sneaked around the curtains. The man who worked here had no great interest in the world outside. Was he inflicting punishment on himself?

Tubby went looking for Flowers.

There was a bathroom at the top of the stairs. Its door hung open, revealing walls tiled in pink. A stained white curtain covered a little window. Tubby moved past that private spot and found Flowers poking around in the priest's bedroom.

It, too, was simple enough. A single bed, properly made up, a tidy bedside table with a goose neck lamp, a towering dark mahogany dresser, and prints on the wall of religious figures, all men, some with halos. All were totally unknown to Tubby who, unlike Flowers, was a Protestant.

Even though the old fanatic had abandoned Tubby to be eliminated, the lawyer had the sense that there was something sacrilegious about invading the priest's private space.

"Let's get out of here, man," he whispered to the detective, who was on his knees looking under the bed. "This doesn't feel right."

"Wait just a second," Flowers said, his voice muffled under the mattress. "What have we here?"

He backed out, dragging with him a long plastic bin, the kind that might store extra blankets or winter sweaters. It rolled on little wheels.

"Looks like papers of some kind." He pushed it in Tubby's direction. "There's another one under here." The top half of the detective disappeared again.

Plastic clamps fastened each end of the bin, and Tubby wasted no time popping them open. Inside were dozens of neatly stacked file folders and ledger books, packed tightly next to each other. Tubby extracted the first one on top.

The folder was labeled, "March 1961." Inside were carbon copies of "Minutes," and on the first sheet he saw, after the date and a list of names who were "In Attendance," a "Discussion of Castro Nationalizing Church Property." He gave it a quick read, which revealed that the discussion detailed efforts to lobby Florida Senator Smathers and Louisiana Senator Long for military intervention in Cuba.

Flowers dragged out the other box. Tubby grabbed it and looked inside. On top was a folder labeled "March 25, 1963." And the first item, also called "Minutes," stated that, "The application of Lee H. Oswald is tabled. Donation of $200 from Judge Perez accepted. Bookkeeper will acknowledge." Tubby replaced the cover on the bin.

"This could be very heavy stuff," he said hoarsely.

"We can carry them."

"That's not what I meant," Tubby said.

"Want to take them?" Flowers asked.

The lawyer pondered. The material wasn't theirs, of course, but it had unmistakable historical significance. This priest and his friends had possibly killed a police officer to keep it hidden. And it was stuff that Tubby would really like to read.

He nodded, and the two men, each carrying one of the long bins, shuffled down the steps.

Flowers clicked off the lights as they went, and they exited from the back. Catching his breath, Tubby waited with the boxes in the driveway, looking as inconspicuous as a stranger can look standing beside a priest's house in a residential neighborhood at two in the afternoon, while Flowers brought the Yukon around. They made quick work of storing the boxes in the back, and both men jumped inside. Flowers circled the block so that Tubby could hop into his own car, and they were out of there.

* * *

The two bins ended up at Tubby's home, which the lawyer deemed the most secure location immediately available.

He searched in his mind for the name of any history scholar he might know, and came up empty. So he called the Dean of the Tulane Law School and asked him to whom he ought to speak about an important collection of Louisiana documents urgently needing preservation.

He got the name of a Dr. Sternwick, who was in charge of

one of the university Library departments, and he called the man right away. Getting a voicemail, Tubby left his name and number, dropping the Dean's name liberally.

Then he took a quick shower.

Peggy O'Flarity had said she might stop in for a glass of wine before driving back to the Northshore, and he had a lot to tell her.

* * *

The morning paper brought the news that Carlos Pancera had died from what appeared to be a self–inflicted gunshot. He was described as "a prominent Latin American civic leader."

Had the disappearance of his files pushed Pancera over the edge? Tubby wondered about that, and also whether someone might have found it expedient to eliminate him. Pancera was survived by a big family.

During the day, Tubby had been leafing through the bins, and Peggy, who had changed her plans and stayed with him, brought coffee. She entertained herself tending to Tubby's bruises, answering emails, and reading the news on her laptop.

"Look at this," she interrupted early in the afternoon, plunking her screen in front of Tubby.

An obituary was posted in the online version of the paper. The reference to "self-inflicted wound" had been deleted entirely. The service was going to be held next Sunday at the St. Agapius Church. It would be performed by 'Father Escobar (ret)'.

"This priest," Tubby said. "I see him talked about in the minutes. Let me read you something." He located one folder from the pile. "October 15, 1963," he read. "It says: 'The Special Mission to Texas is underway.' Could they be talking about killing the President? And at the end it says: 'Our work was blessed by the Night Watchman.' "

"And you think... what?" she asked.

"It's plain," Tubby said. "Who else would give the bene-diction but a priest? I think I've found the 'Night Watchman!' "

XXIX

Peggy left later that afternoon. She had children coming in the morning to ride the horses and she had to get ready for them. Tubby regretted her departure. He had enjoyed their unexpected night together, in his house, and appreciated her concern for his injuries. Now the place felt empty. He looked around the kitchen and found that the refrigerator was also empty. Making a quick mental list of things he needed to pick up at Langensteins, he grabbed his keys.

While locking the front door, he noticed a silver Chevy Impala parked under the live oak tree shading the curb. His own car was in the driveway, but as he walked toward it, the driver's door of the Impala opened and out stepped Detective, or retired detective, Kronke.

Tubby turned to face him and dropped his ring of keys into his pocket to free up his hands. Kronke, ever the cop, marched in like he owned the place and planted himself less than a foot away from the homeowner's shoe tips. Kronke was shorter and rounder than Tubby, but he had a lot of muscle mass packed under his blazer. He was bald and red-faced. He had the remains of a fat cigar stuck in the corner of his mouth.

"You got a lot of nerve," he said to Tubby, punching out the words.

"What the heck are you talking about?" the lawyer asked, his butt braced against the door of his Camaro.

"Walking around like you ain't got a care in the world. You ain't forgot where you was two nights ago have you?"

Tubby wasn't sure what Kronke knew or didn't know, so he just said, "What's it to you?"

"I'm asking the questions." Kronke pointed a finger as if to prod the lawyer in the stomach but stopped, maybe sensing Tubby balling up his fists. "Tell me how you killed Rick Sandoval."

"I don't know what you're talking about."

"How'd you pull that off?"

"I want you to get the hell off my property."

"Listen to me, you dumb shit. Your days are numbered and that number is going to get a lot smaller if you cause any more trouble for the Pancera family."

"What's it to you? I thought it was your father who investigated the Parker kid's murder."

"You happen to be messing with my friends."

"So you were in the group, too? What did they call you? The 'Cop's Kid'?"

"It's none of your business."

"How about Sandoval? You called him 'Security,' right?"

"He's never been anything but an FBI snitch," Kronke grunted.

That shut Tubby up.

"You got it?" Kronke mocked him. "You killed a government man."

"Did I save you the trouble?" Tubby whispered.

Kronke's grin was mean. "That's something you can worry about at night, Dubonnet. In the meantime, leave my friends alone."

"You mean friends like their priest, Escobar?"

"Him, especially," Kronke growled, edging forward until their chests almost touched.

"What was his job in the group? Father Confessor?"

"You're a shithead." His breath was in Tubby's face.

"Did they call him the 'Night Watchman'?"

"Now you're going too far." Kronke reached into his jacket as if going for a shoulder pistol, but Tubby's fist caught him in the jaw.

Kronke stumbled back and came up with a gun, but not before Tubby drew down on him with his own .45.

Panting deeply, the lawyer still managed to get out, "I'm entitled to shoot to kill anyone who threatens me on my property. You know that, old man?"

Kronke straightened up and carefully re-holstered his pistol. He felt his jaw, then spat onto the driveway near Tubby's shoe. He grinned, wiped his lips slowly, turned around, and walked away. His car screeched off down the quiet street.

One of Tubby's neighbors came out on her front porch to see who was causing trouble, and Tubby promptly hid his weapon. He got behind the wheel, still shaking.

Once he remembered what he was doing, he drove off to the grocery store.

* * *

The next morning, while Tubby's new girlfriend was giving horse rides to happy children in some better place, Tubby was pulled away from his second cup of coffee by the ringing house phone.

He didn't recognize the voice that asked for Mr. Dubonnet, but the caller explained.

"My name is Victor Argueta. I'm a policeman. I've been

investigating the shooting of an officer named Ireanous Babineaux."

"I thought that was being handled by Internal Affairs. Is that you?"

"So you knew Babineaux?"

"Yes. He was my client."

"That's what I gathered."

"Really? How?"

"From his text messages. I downloaded them off his phone."

"Great initiative," Tubby said.

"Not really. It's not very hard."

"It's impressive that you thought to do it."

"Not all cops are stupid, Mister Dubonnet. In fact, most of us aren't."

"Sorry. I've just had some bad experiences in the last few days with members of the force."

"Understood. Did one of those happen to be Archie Alonzo?"

"The head of your union?"

"The head of the union, yeah."

"No. I've never met him. Why do you ask?"

"There was a text from Alonzo that could be interpreted as a threat to Babineaux."

"They weren't on the best of terms. Alonzo claimed that my client broke his jaw."

"That's right. Your client did, in fact, break his jaw. That could be reason enough to kill a man, don't you think?"

"Could be. Or to have him killed. Is that what happened?"

"I don't know. How about Rick Sandoval?"

"The cop who got blown up? What about him?"

"Babineaux sent him a text, asking him to help you find some documents."

"That's right. Sandoval located an old police file for me,

about a shooting that happened in the 1970s. He didn't find much."

"Closed file, huh? A lot of those are very skimpy. Officer Babineaux also texted Alonzo and told him to stay out of the business, by which I think he meant the off-duty patrolman referral service. It was a racket that Babineaux and Sandoval were running."

"I didn't know it was a 'racket.' "

Officer Argueta chuckled into the phone. "It was a way to make lots of money off cops who need to make a little money. But I guess it was probably legit. Alonzo has it all to himself now."

"What does that tell you?"

"I got two dead cops. Ireanous Babineaux and Rick Sandoval, both of them twenty-year veterans, like me. And one thing that links them together is Archie Alonzo."

"That's interesting."

"I think so. But guess what? The other thing that links them together is you."

Tubby couldn't argue with that.

But he wasn't ready to spill what he knew about the youth group, Pancera, and all those old records. Not to a stranger on the telephone, and not while those papers were still in his house.

He placed another call to the Tulane historian, but he got the same voice mail.

"These university guys work less than I do," he muttered to himself.

He decided to devote a few more hours to going through those bins. His initial foray had taken him up to the fall of 1963.

He fixed another cup of coffee and opened the folder identified as "November 1963 to December 1963." The first papers in it were minutes of a meeting on November 1, 1963.

As usual, the meeting was called to order by "the Leader" and there was a quick report from "Security" to the effect that no new subversives had been identified in New Orleans, other than the usual outside agitators and the fact that a lawyer had arrived from New York City to staff the "Committee for Civil Rights" office on Magazine Street. She would be watched.

Then came a financial report from the Recorder. There had been new income of $35.25 as a result of "paper sales." Then there was a note that "$100 delivered to J. Ruby for Dallas travel plans." Tubby jumped up and began to pace the room. There was only one Ruby he could think of—the anonymous man who had shot to death the president's assassin, Lee Harvey Oswald, in the basement of the Dallas police station, before Oswald could talk.

When he calmed down, Tubby read on.

* * *

"Should I pick you up?" The voice was Peggy's, and it broke Tubby's spell. He tried hard to remember what she was talking about.

"The wine and cheese?" she prompted. "The gallery opening? Dinky Bacon's exhibit on Julia Street? Five o'clock?"

"Yeah, yeah, yeah. I did sort of forget. I've got to grab a quick shower. How about I meet you there?"

"At five," she repeated.

"Right. I'll be there."

* * *

He made it to "Gallery Row" just a few minutes late, wearing a blue linen jacket over a natty white shirt and khakis. After cruising two blocks in both directions he reluctantly accepted

206

valet parking and handed over his keys to a teenager with styled yellow-blond hair. A number of the art galleries were apparently having functions at the same time because the sidewalk was packed with pedestrians, all dressed in good taste and all looking like they had some money to spend.

Through its expansive windows one could see that "The Gallery Z'Herbes" was popular tonight. Tubby adjusted his collar, took a deep breath, and plunged in.

More people than legally allowed were crowding the center of the narrow space, waving glasses of wine and laughing at each other's wit while not paying a lot of attention to the art. Tubby, however, found it hard not to inspect the work, partly because it seemed so inartful. The pieces were smaller than those displayed at the Contemporary Arts Center, but they were of the same genus. The first to catch his attention was an irregular construction of white plastic water pipes from which was suspended a rusty wrench and three framed black-and-white photographs. They depicted what appeared to be old-time Bourbon Street burlesque shows.

Peggy found him studying one of these pictures—girls in a can-can line.

"My forgetful date appears," she said and lightly kissed his cheek. "Our artist is in the back room. He asked if you were coming."

They picked their way around two diminutive men with identical goatees and chartreuse turtlenecks to the next display. "Is his filmmaker with him?" Tubby asked.

"I didn't see him," Peggy said, which was a disappointment to Tubby. He leaned over to admire an ancient cast-iron water heater repurposed as art. A number of framed photographs had been fastened to it with solder. One picture in particular caught his eye.

"This is interesting," he said.

"What is it?"

"Here, take a look."

She bent over, careful not to spill the contents of her plastic cup.

"It's some old building?" she ventured.

"Doesn't that look familiar to you?" They were cheek to cheek. "See that door? See that window? I'm pretty sure that's an old photograph of Janie's bar, the Monkey Business."

"You could be right."

"Look over the door. Doesn't that say 'Club Caragliano'?"

"It could say that. I'd need my glasses." Tubby didn't know that Peggy wore glasses, but never mind.

"And there's a poster on the door." Tubby pushed his nose up to the picture. "I think it says 'Vince Vance and the Valiants. No Cover'."

"Okay. So?" Peggy wasn't getting it.

"What it means," Tubby shouted in his excitement, "is that there was live music in Janie's bar back in the days of Polaroids. She's going to win her case. Let's go find Dinky before he sells this contraption to somebody."

XXX

Cherrylynn's day at the office got off to a bad start. Tubby didn't show up, and he was short with her when she took the initiative and called him to ask if there were any assignments for her.

"Use the time for studying," he said. That was nice, since she was on the clock, but not so nice because studying for eight hours was going to be extremely boring. The ringing telephone gave her hope.

The man's voice at the other end said, "My brother got a call from this number, asking about a boy who disappeared back in the 1970s."

All boredom vanished.

"That was from me. Who's calling, please?"

"This is Mister Haggarty. To whom am I speaking?"

"My name is Cherrylynn. I'm a legal secretary, and my boss Tubby Dubonnet is investigating the shooting of a young man that took place here in New Orleans during that period."

"Shooting, huh? That's what my brother said." The voice was unemotional.

"Yes, a boy who was killed in a demonstration."

"Was it some kind of civil rights protest?"

"No, I think it was against the war."

"Yeah, that sounds like Parker. He was a troubled youth,

not like his kid sister. He didn't seem to want to get along here in Muncie. As soon as he turned seventeen, he hitched a ride out of town. We got one postcard from him about a year later, and it was from New Orleans. After that, we ain't heard a thing."

"Are you his father?"

"Yes, that's right. Spencer R. Haggarty."

"And his name was?"

"Parker M. Haggarty."

"I'm real sorry to say that this could be the same boy. I hate to be the one telling you this news. I can have Mister Dubonnet call you as soon as he comes in. I'm sure he can tell you more."

"No need for that. Parker never wanted us to know his business, and if he's dead, he's dead. If his sister wants, she can call you."

Cherrylynn didn't know what to say.

"Well, you be good," the man said, and he hung up.

XXXI

Tubby finally connected with the Tulane Library and arranged to drop off the bins. With some effort, and help from a passing undergraduate, he hauled them up the steps to the circulation desk. He asked the student behind it to summon Dr. Sternwick. The librarian appeared quickly and helped Tubby move the boxes into one of the offices. The lawyer took a chair and gave the doctor a quick summary of what he thought he had found.

"Do you mean the JFK assassination?" the librarian asked doubtfully.

"Yes," Tubby said. "And more." He popped open one of the plastic covers and flipped open one of the folders that referenced Lee Harvey Oswald.

Sternwick's eyes narrowed as he looked at the pages more closely.

"There's lots more in there," Tubby repeated. "You've got material on Judge Leander Perez down in Plaquemines Parish. There's this money trail to Dallas. There's evidence of shootings and beatings and other crimes. And how the police gave cover to the whole thing."

"How would we authenticate any of this material?" the skeptical librarian wondered out loud.

"I guess you could get together some scholars. I'll tell them what I know and who else they ought to talk to."

"We do have local scholars," Sternwick said, thinking out loud. "There's a Professor Prima over at Loyola. I'll call him right away and tell him what we think we have. And there are, of course, people here at Tulane, too, I'm sure."

Tubby just nodded along. He was content that the wheels were at last beginning to turn.

"How did you get these papers?" the librarian asked.

"That's a long story," Tubby said. "I might want to have my own lawyer in the room when I tell it. But if you decide that these records are real and want to open them up to the world, I'd like to give them a name."

"What's that?"

"I'd call it the 'Parker M. Haggarty Collection.' "

* * *

Since Jason Boaz wouldn't answer his phone, Tubby resorted to beating on the inventor's door.

A timid cry from within asked, "Who's there?" and Tubby told him. He was admitted. Boaz was dressed very properly in a newly-pressed black suit and blue-striped tie.

"Whose funeral?" Tubby asked.

"I'm preparing for my own," Jason said morosely. Tubby followed him back to the kitchen where Boaz had pancakes on the griddle. "I don't know what to make of the world, Tubby," he said and flipped his breakfast onto a waiting china plate. "I think I may be out of place in this space and time."

Tubby took a chair at the small kitchen table. "You have been acting unbalanced, Jason," he acknowledged.

"Yes, I suppose I have."

"You are in a lot of trouble," the lawyer went on. "You killed a policeman, and whoever that other man was with him, the fat one."

"His name is not important, and never was. To us he was just the 'Leader.' "

"And you tried to kill me, and you almost got Raisin."

"You'll get me out of this, won't you, Tubby?" Boaz poured syrup liberally over his pancakes. "You always have."

"I can't be your lawyer this go-round, Jason. That should be pretty obvious."

"Oh well, it probably doesn't matter. He'll catch up with me soon enough."

"Who?"

"The Night Watchman, of course."

"You mean the priest, Father Escobar?"

Jason looked at Tubby as if he were psycho.

"That's a ridiculous idea, Tubby. What does that venial-sinful individual know about shooting policemen, or putting a bomb in a car, for Heaven's sake?" Thinking that he had made a pun, Jason broke out in laughter, which he squelched with a large forkful of his dripping confection.

Tubby was taken aback. "I was sure it was the priest. There was a passage in the minutes where it said that the 'Night Watchman' said the benediction."

"That means nothing," Jason scoffed. "We were all very religious in those days. Any one of us could offer a proper prayer. The task rotated from meeting to meeting."

"So, who did all those things? Who tried to run me off the road in Folsom?"

"I didn't know about that, but can you imagine Father Escobar driving to the Northshore?" Jason scoffed.

"So who was it? Was it always the policeman, Rick Sandoval?"

"Rick was very mean," Boaz said sadly. "May he rest in peace. No, Rick couldn't be every place at once. He was a working man with a schedule to keep."

"So who was it? Who was the Night Watchman? Who killed Parker Haggarty?"

"There were generations of Night Watchmen."

"Never mind that. Who killed Parker Haggarty?"

"Paul Kronke, of course. Our other faithful policeman. And he may kill me for telling you."

"Detective Kronke?" the lawyer was flabbergasted. "Why, he's not even Cuban."

"Naturally not," Jason said, spreading his hands. "No Cuban would be so brutish and, what's the word, unsubtle."

* * *

"He said it was Detective Kronke, now retired," Tubby told Raisin. They had taken a table at Janie's bar on St. Claude. The place was dead. They were the only customers in it. "Sandoval was apparently Kronke's mentor and preceded him onto the police force by about a year. Because of Kronke's family connections on the force, they could both be instrumental in keeping the youth group and its activities protected."

"Doesn't sound like a Latin name to me," Raisin said. "Kronke, what's that?"

"I don't know. German, maybe. Jason just said that Kronke's family was very anti-Communist. Actually, he said, 'anti-Bolshevik.' The youth group appealed to all kinds."

"Probably an FBI plant."

"What do you mean?"

"Don't you remember? In those days the most rabid provocateurs were actually undercover FBI agents."

"The funny thing is," Tubby said, "Kronke made the same accusation about Rick Sandoval."

"Really? Did you tell Jason Boaz that he may have blown up an undercover agent?"

"Yes, I did. He said it couldn't be true. He even laughed about it. Then he started crying. That's when I left him."

"A movement rife with CIA and FBI men is certainly an interesting proposition, but how would we ever know?"

"We won't. And we've got a bigger problem than figuring that out."

"What's that."

"Kronke is still on the loose." Tubby stared at the wall, trying to imagine what further mayhem the retired homicidal detective might still be capable of. "You know," the morose lawyer continued, "there is evil out there."

"That's where I've always questioned you, buddy," Raisin complained. "Statements just like that."

"You disagree?"

"No—but I wouldn't say it."

"Because it's too true?" Tubby was insistent.

"No, because it just doesn't sound grown up."

Tubby was offended. "Well, what if I said it this way? The world is depressingly full of mindless brutality."

"That's a lot better."

"And the worst of that brutality is committed by the male half of the population," Tubby mused.

Raisin slouched in his chair. "Now you're getting too philosophical," he said.

"You disagree with that?"

Raisin shrugged. "The record is pretty clear, but I'd have to add something, based on my own life's experiences."

"What's that?"

"You can't just put it all on 'the men' or on 'the world.' " He put quotation marks around the words with his fingers. "Sometimes the bad stuff is committed by each of us."

"As in you and me?"

"I'm not excluding anybody."

"You want a drink?" Tubby asked.

"Not at this very moment." Knowing him as well as he did, Tubby figured what he wanted was a cigarette. "Has your determination to nail the guy who killed that boy Parker been satisfied?" Raisin asked, evidently to change the subject.

"No. It's not over yet. Sandoval, Pancera, and the fat man are all gone, that's true. But the others in the car, that priest, Escobar, and Detective Kronke, who pulled the trigger, haven't yet been brought to justice."

"How do you plan to do that?"

"I think the papers I gave to Tulane will hang them." Tubby's spirits revived just thinking about it.

"What about Jason Boaz?"

"I'm not sure." Tubby frowned. "I reckon he kept me from being beaten to death at the warehouse."

"After he tried to kill you with a bomb."

"There's that."

"And you know he committed a murder. He blew up Rick Sandoval."

"There's that, too. Maybe he's insane," Tubby said hopefully.

"I doubt that." Raisin wasn't buying it. "He's just a wicked dude."

"Didn't you just say we're all evil?"

"Not all the time. Just on special occasions."

"Hell, I'm going to have a drink."

"Ok. I'll join you."

Tubby rapped on the table to wake up Jack, who had been dreaming about hiking in the Gifford Pinchot National Forest.

The street door opened and a burly man with a fringe of white hair was silhouetted by the sun.

Raisin recognized the neighbor with whom he'd shared Maker's Mark the week before.

"Mr. Monk!" he called out.

The man looked about slowly, taking the place in, before he decided to approach them.

"Hello," Raisin said. "This is my friend, Tubby Dubonnet. Have a seat with us."

"Don't mind if I do. They call me Monk," Monk said. He pulled out a wooden chair and squared himself away in the seat.

"What are you drinking?" Raisin asked.

"I'll do the same as before," their guest said obligingly.

Jack came over and all three men ordered different concoctions.

"First time I've been in here in twenty years," Monk observed. He looked around to reacquaint himself with the room. "I saw your car outside," he added, meaning Raisin's sporty ride.

"What do you think of it?" Raisin asked.

"It ain't changed much," he said with approval. "It's not too bad when it's quiet like this."

"Has the noise problem gotten any better?"

"Maybe a little." Monk accepted his glass and took a deep swallow. "But not all the way better."

Tubby took a sip. "Maybe there's something we could do to work that out," he suggested quietly.

Monk eyed him suspiciously. "Maybe," he said. "Like what? And who's 'we'?"

"I'm just thinking out loud," Tubby said, staring into his glass. "Maybe a free bar tab on whatever your favorite afternoon is. Something along those lines. You know, for being a good neighbor and keeping an eye on the place in the daytime. I said 'we' because I'm the owner's lawyer."

"Could maybe work something out," Monk took another swallow, "along those lines. You say you're a lawyer?"

"Yes, I am," Tubby acknowledged.

"Is that right? Well, listen, I've got this legal problem you might want to hear about."

Tubby rubbed his eyes. Raisin broke out laughing and raised his glass to toast the table.

* * *

In the moonlight, parked at the Fly where Audubon Park touches the black void of the Mississippi River, three men were having a quiet conversation. It did not worry them that the park was closed and empty, except for the animals asleep in the zoo. Two of the three carried a badge.

"I'm not going to miss either of those cops, Babineaux or Sandoval," Archie Alonzo said. He pronounced each word carefully so they could be understood through the brace which had been clamped around his neck to support his jaw.

"I wouldn't think so," Trey Caponata agreed. "More pie for us."

"That's what it's all about, right? I've still got a union to run."

"So long as you provide uniformed officers to guard all my private functions, we'll get along just fine," Caponata said.

"It's going to be easier than it was before," Alonzo assured him. "My eventual goal is to privatize the whole police force. Run it just like a business."

"A legitimate business," Detective Kronke added. "Where everybody pays for what they get."

"The cops will end up better off in the long run," Alonzo insisted through his brace. "They'll make lots more money."

"If you want police protection, you ought to pony up for it," Caponata added, laughing. "The more you pay, the more you get."

"And I'll be in charge of seeing that everybody pays their

rightful share!" Kronke announced triumphantly. He might be old, but he definitely knew how to get things done.

* * *

Though some of the bad guys were still out there, Tubby was feeling victorious on all fronts. To a large degree, the Parker Haggarty murder had been avenged and, in short order, the remaining perpetrators would almost certainly be exposed and convicted for their past crimes. Maybe history would even be rewritten when the "Haggarty Collection" was made public.

The Monkey Business bar now had the upper hand in its dispute with the city, though no one could ever predict what twists and turns New Orleans zoning politics could take. And Dinky Bacon's electric and trendy career had survived its run-in with heretofore unknown public obscenity laws. They were even thinking about doing an article about him in *The New Yorker* magazine.

In a good mood, enjoying the spectacle of a Lykes 20,000-ton container ship far below his window carefully navigating the riverbend at Algiers, Tubby decided to do something he always professionally avoided—solicit—no, almost solicit—a client. But since Jane Smith had certainly been wronged, probably needed help, and almost certainly wouldn't pay him, this might be all right, if he was very subtle about it.

He banished his doubts and called the quality-of-life officer on her cell.

"This is Tubby Dubonnet," he told her when she answered. "You may remember me."

"Right. I do. The lawyer." Her voice was flat.

"That's me. A lot has happened since we last spoke about the Monkey Business bar."

"That has nothing to do with me now. I've got a desk job at headquarters."

"Is that a good or a bad thing?"

"I'll deal with it," she said.

"I'm sure you will. You seemed quite competent to me."

"Thanks. I've got some charges going on with Internal Affairs. You don't handle that kind of stuff, do you?"

Ah, the opening he had hoped for.

"I handle just about everything, Officer Smith," he said with conviction. "Would you like to talk about it?"

"I don't know." She sounded weary, as if resigned to an unfavorable outcome in life. "It's probably nothing you would be interested in. It has to do with my sex…"

"Tell you what," Tubby interrupted. "I have a very proficient assistant named Cherrylynn Resilio. How about if I put her on. I'll hop off. But if she thinks you've got a case I'll take a look at it. If she green-lights it, I'm very sure we can help."

"Okay, I'm not doing much of anything else right now."

Tubby put her on "HOLD."

"Cherrylynn," he yelled. "Pick up!"

Given a chance to work its wonders, the law would bring justice to the realm.

* * *

Four men wearing vests identifying them as Entergy electricians entered the Tulane University Library through the service entrance. The men weren't locals, but they had acquired a plan of the building and were quickly able to disable the alarm system. They knew that the campus police were elsewhere, responding to a call regarding rowdy students carousing outside The Boot. At this late hour, the campus was dark and deserted.

Within two minutes they had reached the main floor and located the office of the special collections director. The plastic bins were locked within, as expected, but the lock was quickly overcome. Within five minutes, the men had the bins downstairs, out the back door, and stowed in their waiting van. They pulled cautiously onto Freret Street and drove away with their secret cargo into the peaceful New Orleans night.

THE END

HOW ABOUT A FREE BOOK?

**Keep up to date on terrific new books,
and get a freebie at the same time!**

**First click <u>here</u> to join our mailing list and get
*Louisiana Hotshot!***

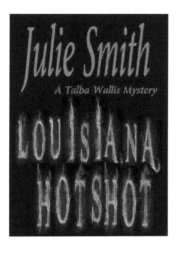

Confirmed grump Eddie Valentino placed the ad. Hotshot twenty-something Talba Wallis knew exactly how to answer it.

And thus was born the dynamic duo of New Orleans private detectives, one cynical, sixty-five-year-old Luddite white dude with street smarts, and one young, bright-eyed, Twenty-First century African-American female poet, performance artist, mistress of disguise, and computer jock extraordinaire. Think Queen Latifah and Danny DeVito in a hilariously rocky relationship—yet with enough detective chops between them to find Atlantis.

***** 5.0 out of 5 stars **Julie Smith's Triumphant Return**
Long time fans of Julie Smith's witty mysteries will not be disappointed by this new title. Spinning off a character from her latest Skip Langdon mystery *"82 Desire"*, Talba Wallis, this book definitely ranks up there with Smith's Edgar Award winning *"New Orleans Mourning."*

WE GUARANTEE OUR BOOKS…
AND WE LISTEN TO OUR READERS

We'll give you your money back if you find as many as five errors. (That's five *verified* errors—punctuation or spelling that leaves no room for judgment calls or alternatives.) If you find more than five, we'll give you a dollar for every one you catch up to twenty. More than that and we reproof and remake the book. Email mittie.bbn@gmail.com and it shall be done!

Want to start at the beginning?

**The first Tubby Dubonnet mystery is
CROOKED MAN.**

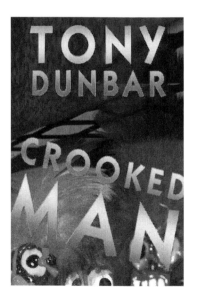

http://amzn.to/19zuVM4

What they said about CROOKED MAN:

"The wacky but gentle sensibilities of Tubby Dubonnet reflect the crazed, kind heart of New Orleans better than any other mystery series."

—*The New Orleans Times-Picayune*

"Sharp and jolly ... There's a lot here to enjoy—especially some great moments in local cuisine and a wonderfully jaundiced insider's view of a reluctant lawyer in action."

—*Chicago Tribune*

"Take one cup of Raymond Chandler, one cup of Tennessee Williams, add a quart of salty humor, and you will get something resembling Dunbar's crazy mixture of crime and offbeat comedy."

—*Baltimore Sun*

Also by Tony Dunbar:

The Tubby Dubonnet Series (in order of publication)

CROOKED MAN
CITY OF BEADS
TRICK QUESTION
SHELTER FROM THE STORM
CRIME CZAR
LUCKY MAN
TUBBY MEETS KATRINA
NIGHT WATCHMAN

Other Works by Tony Dunbar

American Crisis, Southern Solutions: From Where We Stand,
    Promise and Peril
Where We Stand: Voices of Southern Dissent
Delta Time
Our Land Too
Against the Grain: Southern Radicals and Prophets, 1929-1959
Hard Traveling: Migrant Farm Workers in America

A Respectful Request

We hope you enjoyed *Night Watchman* and wonder if you'd consider reviewing it on Goodreads, Amazon (http://amzn.to/19zsqt2),
or wherever you purchased it. The author would be most
grateful.

About the Author

TONY DUNBAR is a lawyer who lives in New Orleans, the mirthful and menacing city in which the Tubby Dubonnet mystery series is set. In addition to the mysteries, which have been nominated for the Anthony Boucher and the Edgar Allan Poe awards, he is also the Lillian Smith Book Award-winning author of books about the South, civil rights and protest. He has an abiding interest in the Battle of New Orleans and other grand dramas in the city's colorful history and imaginative culture.

Printed in Great Britain
by Amazon